'94

DRAGON MOON

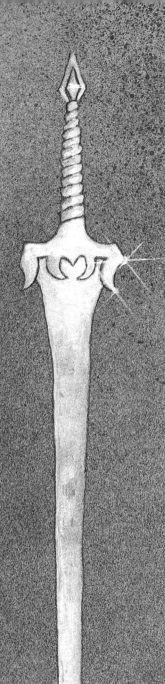

DRAGO

CHRIS CLAREMONT
AND
BETH FLEISHER

Illustrations by JOHN BOLTON

BANTAM BOOKS

NEW YORK   TORONTO   LONDON   SYDNEY   AUCKLAND

DRAGON MOON
A Bantam Book / December 1994

Book design by Maria Carella and John Bolton

Library of Congress Cataloging-in-Publication Data

Claremont, Chris, 1950–
    Dragon moon : the chronicles of the black dragon / Chris Claremont
  & Beth Fleisher ; illustrations by John Bolton.
     p. cm.
  ISBN 0-553-37448-6. — ISBN 0-553-09700-8 (deluxe ed.)
  I. Fleisher, Beth. II. Title.
  PS3553.L255D73   1994
  813'.54—dc20   94-15157
                                    CIP

Published simultaneously in the United States and Canada

Bantam Books are published by Bantam Books, a division of Bantam Doubleday Dell Publishing
Group, Inc. Its trademark, consisting of the words "Bantam Books" and the portrayal of a rooster,
is Registered in U.S. Patent and Trademark Office and in other countries. Marca Registrada.
Bantam Books, 1540 Broadway, New York, New York 10036.

PRINTED IN THE UNITED STATES OF AMERICA
KPH   0 9 8 7 6 5 4 3 2 1

To Lynn and all the gang at the Pensic War
At long last
this one's for you
—C.C.

To R. W.
For all his years of friendship
—B.F.

For Noëlle
—J.B.

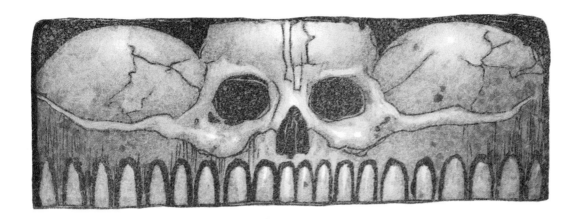

Officially, the War wasn't supposed to start till Friday, but already several dozen cars had beaten her to the bumpy, puddle-strewn turnoff that led to the campground. Cass shook her head as she glared at the queue ahead and seriously considered turning back. Problem was, another car had pulled in behind her; effectively she was trapped. She crashed through the lower gears of her GTi, biting her lip to keep from shouting out the window exactly what she thought of the driving skills of the idiot in the Toyota one up the line. It had been fifteen years since her first War, and she thought it might be that she was finally too old for it all.

Just what I need, she grumped to herself as she slammed into second and rode his bumper up to the admissions gate, *more damn fools than usual eager to try their luck and make their bones.* By trying their very best to break hers.

Cass handed back her signed waiver (which said, in effect, that if she was dumb enough to get herself seriously hurt or even killed this weekend, it was her own bloody fault) and eased her GTi around the handful of vehicles crowding the entrance to the sprawling campground. She didn't see anyone she knew near the registration tent. Hardly surprising. Most of her friends weren't due till week's end, saddled now as they were with the responsibilities of work and family.

Easier way back when, she thought. *We just threw the gear in the car and hit the road. No muss, no fuss, no worries.*

She crossed the old wooden bridge—marveling as always at how it took the weight of her car and wondering how it would handle the RVs yet to come—and started along a dirt track labeled the HIGH ROAD; according to his fax, George and

1

the others planned to be in their usual spot by the tree line at the opposite end of the field, roughly a quarter mile distant. She crept in first gear the whole way, using the torque to push through the thick mud created by almost a week's worth of late spring rain. She had to brake more than once for people and other cars, muttering under her breath at the burgeoning popularity of the War.

She had a pickup tape that alternated Hendrix and vintage Doors in the cassette deck—his guitar and Morrison's bourbon baritone had been joyously sizzling her brain for the last hour, with "Riders on the Storm" now vibrating the windshield of the VW. But both were as out of place here as she was beginning to feel, so she yanked that tape in favor of Battlefield Band's *Homeground*.

She didn't understand her mood; she'd been in a funk for days. If the others hadn't been depending on her, if she hadn't had fifteen years (*My god*, she thought, *fifteen years!*) of tradition (*Or was it inertia?*) behind her, she might well have stayed home. Was it summer doldrums, global warming, midlife crisis? The more she thought about it, the worse things got; the harder she tried *not* to think about it, the more she did.

Even work didn't help. This past fortnight, she'd functioned on autopilot, producing solid, dependable scripts with barely the slightest awareness of what the stories were about. Her editor was satisfied, but Cass knew that in four months, when the comics went on sale, she'd read them and be appalled. What disturbed her more was that she didn't give much of a damn about that, either. This spring, nothing seemed to matter.

A burly teenager in a not terribly well-crafted Roman legionnaire's kilt, sandals, and a spear loomed in front of the car and waved her to an abrupt halt.

"Better not go any farther, milady," he told her, leaning in her open window.

"Why not?" she demanded.

"The rain. This is the first decent day in a week. You think the road behind poots, you're in for a revelation. Totally the pits. You drive in, you won't get out. We've had to tow a bunch of cars already. We've been laying down straw for traction, but what it really needs is a good hit of sun."

"Shit." This posed no real problem. If the camp was where it was supposed to be, she wouldn't have to hump her gear far, but after a day of traveling, the inconvenience wasn't something she looked forward to.

"Precisely. Sorry," he added, seeing her scowl.

"Not your fault, it's been that kind of day."

"Cheer up. There'll be dancing in the Barn later this evening— Hey, aren't you Cass Dunreith? I mean"—he cleared his throat and tried to drop his voice an octave—"beg pardon, Lady Siobhan of Craigsmere?"

He used her Society name, but Cass nodded and said, "Cass is fine. Actually, I'm thinking of retiring the Siobhan persona."

"I hope that doesn't mean you won't fight in the Champion's Combat. I saw you last year, you were awesome!"

"I lost."

"You wuz robbed. You should be King this War." He looked quickly around, as though for eavesdroppers, and pitched his words for her alone. "Not Fieran."

"He wanted the damn job."

Cass put her car into gear, willing the tires to grab despite the mud, surprised at how tender a nerve the boy had touched. She'd picked up a bug last War, and fought in between bouts of nausea. It was a tribute to her raw skill that she still managed to reach the final round, but that was where luck and strength ran out. It galled her, the way she lost, didn't feel quite right then or now. She didn't want to be King, didn't like the bureaucratic nonsense that went with the title, didn't need the ego boost from the perpetual coterie of brown-nosed sycophants determined to attach themselves to the reigning monarch. Fieran, though—strange, how she always found it hard to think of him as anything other than his Society persona— enjoyed it all too much.

The boy bravely shouted after her, "I hope you fight this year. A lot of us hope you win!"

She bumped and skidded along the road, then pulled off and parked on a solid patch of grass that was as close as she dared go to the camp. She'd gone only a couple of steps before her sneakers squished ankle-deep in muck. Springing aside with a loud curse, she barely kept her balance as she found herself tangled in an ankle-high rope border that had been stretched between wooden stakes to claim a campsite.

"Hail the prodigal daughter," a familiar voice called.

"Bleedingbloody*hell*!" she replied.

George opened his arms wide and gathered her in; she let him take her weight, which didn't bother him at all. She was tall, a couple of inches shy of six feet, but he towered above her, with the broad shoulders, thick, bushy beard, and booming laugh that went with his Viking persona. He was in garb: sandals, homespun linen trousers, and loose cotton shirt, and she could see his armor scattered in front of his tent.

"Thanks," Cass breathed, "I needed that."

"Thought so. What the hell happened to your hair?" he squawked, taking a good look at her.

She rubbed a hand across her close-cropped scalp. "It seemed like a good idea at the time," she told him sheepishly. She'd worn her hair long all her life. A couple of Wars ago, it had fallen, straight and raven black, almost to her knees. But now, with barely an inch of it left, the effect was bullyboy tough, with a random dusting of silver as a harbinger of age. "I just got tired of lugging all that weight around. I have to admit, for summer in New York this is a lot more comfortable."

"If you say so. Me, I say it's a desecration. Want some help with your stuff?"

"I can handle things, Rags, there's no need. . . . "

"H'every knight needs a squire, milady." He spoke with a remarkably precise, Monty Python Brit accent.

She responded in kind. "Roight! For the record"—she raised her voice, turning a few nearby heads—"I want it known by all ye present that it's *your* fault, Faraday, *you* started it this time! *I* was all prepared to talk like a normal person." Without missing a beat, she shifted into broad Highlander Scots. "But you had to go an' set me off. Be it on yuir head, then."

He was laughing. "I should've known. That's very good, you been practicing?"

She shook her head. "Just doing what comes naturally."

"Yeah, well, you were born there, that gives you an unfair advantage." She made a rude face and tossed her tent at him from the open hatch of the car.

"Ah-*ha*!" George switched to faultless Hollywood Indian, an accent that Cass had tried time and again to match before finally conceding she couldn't even come close. "Oh my goodness gracious me, memsahib, I do so believe that gives you a terribly unfair advantage over this unworthy person, oh yes indeedy I do." As usual, by the time he was done she was convulsed with laughter.

The second trip, he saw her computer. "What's with?" he asked.

"The usual last-minute panics."

"You couldn't get five days clear?"

"Mine is a collaborative medium, pal, and when your collaborator screws up, somebody's got to eat the time." She shrugged. "It isn't like this hasn't happened before. Or won't again."

"What a life."

"Beats working. Anyone else here yet?"

"Bosche and Lynn are problematic. Lynn's deadlines are as implacable as yours and her boss a lot less flexible. Dani's due tomorrow, but Tom and Nina canceled. The twins are sick."

"Anything serious?"

"Enough to make the schlep not worth the effort."

"Is it my imagination, Rags, or are we all becoming terribly *respectable*?"

"You mean, in our rapidly approaching dotage? What's the new acronym, Cass, GRUMPs—'Grown-Up, Middle-Aged Professionals'?" He shrugged with mock fatalism. "Hey, we were warned it would happen, we just figured it never would happen to us. How come you're alone? Wasn't Rick . . . ?"

"Didn't work out."

"Sorry."

"Me, too. I figured this time I'd struck gold."

"Want to talk about it?"

4

"Nope. Gimme a hand putting up the tent, will you?"

Before starting, she did a Girl Scout change, sliding on a pair of shorts she'd stuffed into her shoulder bag and pulling off her skirt. There hadn't exactly been a fight between herself and Rick, not then, not ever; it wasn't in his nature, the passive-aggressive sonovabitch. They'd gone to dinner at the Museum Café, and where she'd been ready to suggest they move in together, he'd suddenly announced that he was going to the Coast. A job in L.A., good money, better prospects. He wanted her to come with him. She couldn't. He didn't buy that.

"You're scared," he said, staring glumly at her food as though he wanted it for himself. Cass had to restrain the urge to throw the plate in his face.

"Of what?"

"Us, I think. Me. A commitment."

"Because I won't chuck everything I've worked for to follow you across the bloody country? That's cute."

"Why not? You fax most of your work to the office anyway."

"With the crash schedule I'm on, I need to be in New York. Three hours makes a big difference. Not to mention the fact that I hate Los Angeles with a passion. Then there's my house; not like I could pack it up and bring it with me. Why don't you chuck your job for me, Rick? Aren't *I* worth it?"

"Maybe I want to have what you've got. Maybe I'm tired of taking second place to your work. Y'know, Cass, I have things to prove to myself, and I can't do it in competition with you! I mean, Jesus Christ, woman, they're only comic books!"

"Fuck you," she said with a flat coldness that surprised them both. Without another word, she got to her feet and strode out the door, not bothering to look back as she hailed a cab, wondering if he'd follow, partly hoping he would so she could knock him down. She wanted to hurt him, and was terrified of how far she'd go once she started. She'd never felt such icy rage.

Home in Brooklyn, in the brownstone she'd bought to share with someone— hoping these past months it would be him—she went through a pack of cigarettes and four fingers of her best Aberlour malt in front of the tube, without the slightest notion what of she was watching, or any reaction to it. The phone didn't ring. The next morning she drew red lines through Rick's entry in her Filofax.

That was May, five weeks ago, ancient history.

She stood in the stuffy shadows of the tent and stared down at her suitcase and duffel bag, trying to figure out what to do next. Unpack, of course, but where to begin? She collapsed onto her futon mattress and let the afternoon heat bake into her. With door and window flaps closed, the tent was like a sauna, but for the moment Cass preferred privacy to comfort. She flopped her left arm into view and gazed blearily at her watch; if past experience and the state of the newly constructed fire pit in the center of the campsite were any judge, dinner would be a long time coming.

She could nap for a couple of hours and not be missed. Even as she considered the proposition her body decided for her; when George peeked in to see if she wanted a beer or something cool to drink, she was fast asleep.

⚱

She hears a scream and around her all is bathed in red, roaring light. Flames, she realizes; the camp is on fire. People are running helter-skelter, and there are massively armored figures on equally monstrous horses riding them down. She sees swords and blood and stag-helmed riders, is just about to run for the safety of the trees when a rider points her way and spurs his mount into a thundering gallop. He has a lance. She sees George's wooden buckler splinter under the impact of a true war ax and feels tears fall as he falls, dead. The ground slips out from under her and she sprawls in the mud, yelling in mingled rage and terror—but not, to her surprise, pain—as the steel-tipped lance punches through her breastbone—

⚱

"Cass, you okay?" It was George, kneeling beside her bed, features hidden by the darkness of the evening but concern evident in his voice. She was shaking, her skin clammy with sweat, heart racing fit to burst. She'd had nightmares, but never anything as vivid as this. She felt displaced; it was hard to believe she was alive, George was alive, the campground as peaceful and still as could be.

"A dream," she murmured, not really convinced. "I was dreaming."

"Sounded pretty hairy."

"A dream only a shrink could love—Jesus, it's cold!" Even though it was June, the day's heat vanished with the sun, and a slight breeze was adding a bite to the evening chill.

"It's a little late for just a leotard," George told her, fishing through her gear to find her heavy caracalla cloak to lay across her shoulders. "After all, we're in the mountains."

Cass gathered the cloak around herself as she stepped outside and slumped onto a picnic bench. Another tent had sprung up on their site while she slept. She nodded a bleary hello to Danielle, who was her usual stunning self in a laced black number that managed to fit both the medieval atmosphere of the War and the modern world outside.

"I thought you weren't rolling in until tomorrow?" Cass asked.

"Stefan finished work early, and I decided to play hooky so we could get here tonight."

"And who's Stefan?"

"My new beau." Dani smiled impishly. Ever since Cass had met her the first day of college, Dani had always had a strikingly handsome man somewhere about. She envied Dani her ability to slip in and out of apparently pleasant relationships like so many changes of clothes, especially when she herself had just crashed and burned the last in what seemed an unending stream of bad choices and doomed love affairs.

"So what's this one like?"

"Don't hate me." Dani opened her limpid brown eyes wide to plead with her friend. "Tall, dark, and Hungarian. He made us goulash for dinner. He's off to the Barn, wanted to look around. I'd have gone with him, but one of my costumes needed some fixing up."

"Take me now, Lord." Cass sighed and rolled her eyes. "Bum a cigarette?" she asked Dani, and lit one with a candle flame when she got a nodded yes.

"At least try the goulash," Dani said, handing her a bowl.

"Not hungry, thanks."

"You should eat something, you don't look well."

"Even the thought of it . . ." Cass made a face.

"How about a sip of this?" George handed her a paper cup, then added a splash of brandy. Cass drained it with a swallow, held her hand out for more.

She took her time with the second glass, luxuriating in the liquor's earthy taste, taking comfort in the homely scene of Dani mending a torn skirt and George reading the paper in the light of the fire. Absently she rubbed her breastbone, not quite believing it was whole, thinking of the last image of her dream. She grimaced in embarrassment as she realized that George was looking at her.

"I'm okay," Cass said. "Really."

"Never doubted it for a moment."

She made a face. "Maybe it's the War, or the work I do, my imagination doesn't know when to quit. Especially when I'm exhausted. It's been a helluva spring, Rags."

"What did you see?"

Cass told him, so evocatively that George reached for the brandy and poured himself a shot. The drink made him choke and cough, his expression pulling a chuckle from Cass.

"Don't you dare gloat," he sputtered, and Cass's chuckle became a full-throated laugh.

"I was just remembering homecoming, sophomore year. What was her name?"

"Kimberly." He sighed. "And it was a shame about her shoes. But don't change the subject, Cass Dunreith! Those images are pretty grim."

"Awful, I'd say," offered Dani, with a shiver that wasn't affectation.

"Where do you think they came from?" he asked.

"Schenectady?" Cass lit another cigarette. "It didn't feel like a dream, that's

what's so freaky. Dreams are like soap bubbles that pop as soon as you wake. This one, I can remember every detail. It was more a . . . memory, like déjà vu, something that actually happened."

George looked away nervously. "Yeah, well, there's so many fevered imaginations here in one place, maybe you just tapped into the wrong wavelength."

"Next nap time, I'll try for old episodes of 'Bewitched.' " She rubbed her eyes. "I'm beat."

"You fighting tomorrow?"

"I don't know, George, I guess that's the plan, or I wouldn't have lugged all my gear here." Cass groaned. "It's changed in the last few years. It's not as fun."

"Thanks to that toad-sucking bastard, Fieran. When he saw you weren't at the practice rounds today, he stopped by the campsite and looked inordinately pleased that you weren't here. He said he might even fight for himself this year, instead of using that big hulking sod as his champion."

Cass stood up and slapped George on the back. "All the more reason, Kimo Sabe, for me to get a good night's rest, 'cause I want a piece of him."

⚜

"Wake up, wake up, you sleepy head!
Wake up, wake up! Get out of bed!
The day is young, the boys well hung,
You may be old, but you're not yet dead!"

Cass tried desperately to burrow under her futon to block out the cacophony of spoons banging on pots and the chirping of two unnaturally cheerful voices. She struggled, she pleaded, but they showed no mercy. Grabbing her by wrists and ankles, Lynn and Bosche dumped her on a bench and folded her hands around a mug of steaming coffee.

"You know, guys," Cass croaked, "if this is instant, you automatically die." She took a sip. "French roast, ground beans. You may yet live." She squinted up at her friends, trying to focus on the new arrivals. "Have I slept, not wisely, but too well?"

"Milady Siobhan, surely you must know that I live for the days when I see your beauteous countenance scrubbed fresh by the morning dew." Bosche sketched her a most pretty bow; with his guileless, smiling face and halo of blond curls, Cass wanted to smack him. Instead she turned to Lynn, always the more pragmatic of the couple.

"This is a surprise," she said.

"I got my piece done," was the matter-of-fact reply, followed by a wickedly elfin grin. "We've been driving all night."

"And sampling roadside haute cuisine along the way, no doubt," Cass said. Bosche looked like a Renaissance angel, but his taste was strictly Mickey D's.

"And we have the action figures to prove it!" Lynn snorted, but threw an affectionate look at Bosche.

Cass managed a chuckle that was halfway human, held out her mug for a refill. As she drank she hazarded a squint at the lightening sky.

"Just what time is it, anyway?" she asked.

"Not night, not dawn," George said. "Figure about twenty minutes to sunrise."

"George, I was asleep!"

"You never got your gear together yesterday. You want to miss the Combat?"

"What I want . . . " she began, and then, to her surprise, both thought and desire ran out of gas. She paused, lost in her own head.

"You sure you're up to this?"

"Geez, Rags," she cried in protest, shaking herself awake. "I may be old, but I still kick butt once a week at practice. Just give me some more go juice so I can face this ungodly hour." She held out her mug for another refill.

"This is serious, Cass. I don't trust Fieran."

"What's he going to do, George, poison me? Have me murdered behind the pellements? We're not playing *The Spanish Tragedy*." She took a deep swallow from her mug, aware of just how pissed she sounded.

George doggedly pushed on. "All I'm saying is, don't underestimate him. He's got something to lose this year. He lusts to be High King."

"I should have stayed home. I don't need this, George, I really don't."

"Guys!" Dani interrupted with uncharacteristic force. "With all due respect to you both, enough already! Cass, I think you're too wrapped up in your own head. That's where your nightmare came from."

"It's not, you know," Cass said softly.

"Fine. I don't care. I think the only sane prescription is to take a leaf from yon Viking's book," and she tossed an elegant gesture toward George. "Bugger your analytical self, woman; get physical. Walk out on the Rune Field, kick ass, take names, eat 'em for breakfast. Win or lose, I guarantee you'll feel better." She impaled George with a challenging glare. "Am I right, Faraday, or what?"

"Generally works for me," he said sheepishly. "Cross my heart and—"

"Don't say that!" Cass snapped, making everyone jump. Cass held up her hands and shook her head, a little wild-eyed. "Just getting superstitious in my old age. Now," she said briskly, standing up. "When's the first match?"

"Midmorning," Dani answered. "There's a lot of interest this year, so they had to push the time back to register all the entrants."

"Outstanding," Cass groused. "That was why we kicked the Combat up to the beginning of the week in the first place. What's next—the Champion's Combat in June, the War in July?"

"If you were King," Bosche began, staring thoughtfully at the sky (choosing not to notice the deadly looks from Dani and George, and a solid kick in the shins from Lynn). "If you were King, or even High King, Overlord of all the Domains, then I guess you could change the things that bugged you. Right, Cass?" He looked at her with wide-eyed innocence.

Cass had to laugh. "Point taken. Who's up first?"

"Actually,"—this from George—"you are."

⚜

Royal standards faced off across the meadow, one for each of the four Great Kingdoms who sponsored the War. By week's end, when the campground had grown to the size of a small town, there would be flags galore, declaring Domains large and small, and even individual households. Cass wasn't surprised to note that Fieran's pavilion was the largest and most elaborate. *And such fetching minions!* she thought, but wouldn't dignify them with a glance as she trotted past on the way to her next round.

11

For now, very little mattered to the few-score knights who fought for the privilege to champion their liege lord and win him a kingdom. Not all members of the Society were interested in swinging swords, and even fewer had the dedication to practice and study to earn their knighthood. Most enjoyed the panoply, the dressing up and flirting, but only a few had the honor of wearing spurs.

Quite a bit like the Age of Chivalry, Cass had always thought. She was having herself a grand time, whacking her way up through the list of contenders. She stuffed her uncertainties behind her brazen and bold Highland persona, Lady Siobhan of Craigsmere. She hammed up her accent, playing to the growing crowd who came to watch her matches, reveling in the ego boost that came with each win. Bereft of cold steel, the battles were half theater, and Cass was one knight who never failed to please the audience.

The Champion's Combat was one-on-one, each knight with weapons of his or her choosing. Of course, unlike days of yore, expertise wasn't shown by how much damage one could inflict on an opponent; although accidents did happen, the goal was to demonstrate skill, not brute force. Like fencing, a complex series of points was awarded, based on "touches" and technique. While the matches were physically demanding, all effort was made to avoid real harm. The face was off-limits, knees and groin, too. Armor was mostly pads, weapons were checked for hard edges. Some went for true period re-creations, others created their own style. Her current foe, an old friend hailing from Minneapolis, wore an eclectic mix of classic Japanese and Judaic armor. He was barrel-chested and strong, and knew how to use his body and his weapons to their best advantage. He allowed some blows past his guard because he knew they wouldn't hurt him; his hope was to draw quick-footed Cass off balance. All he wanted was a decent shot at her.

And, with breathtaking suddenness, he had it. She came in too close, too slow, fatigue weighing down her every limb, tainting her every move. He managed to catch her rattan blade. One mailed fist held her blade while the other brought his own faux sword around to administer the *coup de grâce.*

Only she wasn't there to receive it. He'd put the full weight of his body into the blow, pivoting on one solidly braced leg. Cass somehow got behind and beside him, jamming her own hip up against his, pushing him around and over in a perfectly executed judo throw that tumbled him head over heels to the grass.

The next thing he knew, she was standing over him, her sword tucked into her belt, his own pointed at his throat. "Do you yield, Sir Knight?" she asked formally.

"I do so yield to you, Lady. My life and honor are yours," he replied.

Cass grinned, handed him back his sword with one hand, and extended her other to help him up. He was surprised to discover he needed the assistance; the simple effort of clambering to his feet left him gasping.

"Sorry about that," she said, contrition mixing with pride.

"You're sorry? I'd thought I had a fair shot at you this year, Cass."

"Next time, big guy." Her grin lit up her whole face, and she thought just how right Dani had been. The adrenaline rush of combat was exorcising her bogeymen.

"Actually, I could have sworn there were a few times earlier when you had me cold."

Cass nodded and said lightly, "I guess it don't count if the ref don't see 'em."

"You think it's deliberate? Our ref was chosen by His Royal Highness, King Fieran." He shared Cass's opinion of her Domain's ruler.

Cass shook her head. "It's not worth thinking about."

The Master of the Lists hurried over, short of breath from racing from one combat to another. He turned, banged his ceremonial staff twice on the ground, and made the official pronouncement, "A fatal blow has been struck. This combat is ended. I hereby proclaim the rightful victor to be the Lady Siobhan of Craigsmere." Dropping from character, he turned to Cass and slapped her on the back. "Good going, Dunreith. This looks to be your year!"

"Thanks, Peter," she replied, and then threw back her head to give a deafening Highland yell.

Cass accepted congratulations from a whole host of people as she made her way through the crowd toward the tarp her friends had erected under the proud pennant of the helmed computer. Jazzed as she was, she still felt a perceptible drop in temperature when she passed by Fieran's pavilion. *I know, he knows, they all know I want his ass for lunch,* Cass thought with gleeful anticipation. *Then what will that boy do with all his put-on airs?*

Lynn started the applause as Cass drew near, and the others quickly joined in with war whoops and stamping feet, together with some of the casual gathering that pushed close to get a good look at who had won.

" 'See the conquering hero comes! Sound the trumpet, beat the drums.' " Bosche's melodic voice rang out.

Ever pragmatic, Lynn handed Cass a bottle of water.

"Where does he get that stuff?" Cass asked her. "Even I can't place that one."

"His dissertation," Lynn answered indulgently.

Cass snorted, but was too busy chugalugging the water to comment that he'd been working on the damn thing for almost six years. She drained the bottle nearly dry without a break, and then let what remained splash onto her sweat-flushed face.

Sated, Cass looked at her friends. It was a long time since college, but here at least, separated out from the daily demands of work and home, each looked happy. A bit of gray here, a few more pounds there, but all in all Cass thought they had stood up to the test of time. Everyone was in full garb, for a few days letting their imaginations rule their lives. Lynn the no-nonsense journalist wore a peasant blouse with a pretty embroidered bodice over a long, colorful patchwork skirt. It suited her persona of Mélisande, a country girl with too much education, seeking out a little adventure. Bosche favored the faded finery of a ne'er-do-well troubadour with a bell-sleeved shirt, its ribbons left untied and fluttering, and black velvet tights a wish fulfillment away from being quite rude.

"The sneakers are a nice touch," Cass noted. "I like 'em."

For once, Bosche blushed. "I'm still looking for the right boots. I was hoping to find a pair here."

"Oh, Bosche, you're such a shoe slut." Cass shook her head woefully.

"Look who's talking," Lynn chimed. "Besides, black high-tops are appropriate for any age, any occasion."

Cass rolled her eyes. Dani was tucked under the shade of a nearby tree with Stefan. Once again in black, she looked dressed to kill, and he, more than ready to die in her arms.

Cass sensed a solid familiar presence behind her, turned to find George holding out another bottle of water. She was still desperately thirsty but made herself take time with this drink so she wouldn't cramp. The morning's bouts had been preliminaries; she knew the main event was yet to come.

"Not half-bad, kiddo, all things considered," he told her. He looked over her head to Fieran's pavilion and his eyes narrowed, but she decided not to turn and see why.

"The hell you say!" she blustered. "I was bloody marvelous! And getting better all the time."

"Good thing, too. If you win this year, it's not going to be a gift."

"That's a fact." Cass took in that George was out of his armor. "So what happened with you?"

"Some new kid won on points. Only thing, Cass, I swore I had him nailed, and the ref didn't call it." While George didn't have the discipline to make it to the final rounds, he always lasted well into the afternoon's combats. From the frown on his face Cass could tell the defeat didn't sit well with him.

"Look, Rags," she said quietly so only he would hear. "Let's not do this. Let's just have a good time with our friends." He looked her in the eye and nodded; she saw what it cost him and gave him a hug. "Right," she continued in a voice for all to hear, "am I good, or am I good?"

"Oh, modesty," chided Bosche, "thou most becoming of maidenly virtues."

"Nothing immodest about stating a simple fact," she answered tartly, and started to try to remove her armor. George was beside her in a moment, loosening the laces so she could wriggle out of her padded jerkin, working free the knots that held her arm guards in place. "By the by," she continued, studiously casual, "anyone keeping score?"

"You mean, aside from our most dread and gracious liege? Only just about the entire camp," Lynn answered.

Cass collapsed cross-legged on her backside, removing boots first, then greaves and padded pants. "What's the betting line?" she huffed between tugs.

"That it'll be you and Fieran," replied Lynn with displeasure.

"You look to be the main course," George agreed, looking up from where he was making repairs on her armor with duct tape.

Cass rolled over onto her stomach for a gander at Fieran's Royal Pavilion. Folks in expensive costumes milled about, and Cass heard a tinkle of laughter. There was no sign of the King; his courtiers were holding court without him.

"I've been watching," she said. "He was always good; this year, he's better." She rolled back to face the others. "Anyone figure he's hired himself a full-time personal trainer?"

"Isn't that a little extreme?" Lynn asked.

"Isn't his whole approach extreme?" George countered.

"Sad, but true," Cass agreed.

"He uses that spear—"

"It's Japanese, Lynn, a *naginata.*"

The look Lynn gave Bosche shut his mouth with an audible snap. "Whatever," she said, with prim finality. "He uses it like a hockey stick."

"Ideal for amputating limbs, if the blade was steel instead of rubber."

"He's left enough folks sore and limping as it is."

"I know."

Cass clambered to her feet and clapped George across the shoulders. "Not to worry, coach, I'll be careful."

She signaled for Dani and Lynn to hold up a blanket to form an impromptu dressing room. The day was too warm for Lycra tights, so she contented herself with just a fresh tunic of plain linen that fell to her knees, with loose sleeves and no collar for maximum comfort.

"Your advice is working wonders," she told Dani as she laced up her sandals. "I'm grateful."

"Enjoying yourself, are you?" the other woman asked with a smile that made it clear she was.

"So far, so good," Cass answered after a genuine heartfelt laugh. She rose to her feet and settled her new outfit around herself, surveying the field through eyes slitted against the noonday glare. No one was fighting as the camp broke for lunch, and the groundskeepers were going over the field, to prep it for the afternoon. Cass herself felt some pangs of hunger, but she wasn't yet ready to settle down. Her body still sizzled with the jazz of combat.

"I'm for a stroll," she announced.

"You should eat something," George cautioned.

"Don't fret, George, I'll play chaperon," Lynn said cheerily.

Three quick grabs for the last items on her mental list—her sword belt with the pouch containing her wallet and ever-present notebook, a pair of shades, and a wide-brimmed hat—and she was ready. Lynn looked askance at the blade in its scabbard as Cass tweaked its straps so that it hung properly at her hip.

"Steel?" she asked.

"For show," Cass replied. "My arm, gentle Mélisande, is yours."

Beyond the first well-planned line of royal tents was a helter-skelter collection of umbrellas and sunshades sheltering food stalls to feed both combatants and on-lookers. Lynn and Cass were assaulted by a host of good smells, and after a bit of browsing settled on sausage heros and cans of Coke. Someone had done the soft-drink logo in illuminated-manuscript lettering and printed it out on self-stick labels, taking the time to relabel each can. It was impressive work, and the sausages so spicy she and Lynn ended up splitting another can between them as they continued their meander.

It was a beautiful day, with enough people about for two old friends to gal-talk over. Lynn asked after Rick, and when Cass stiffly informed her that he was no longer an issue, Lynn went to work to find her a new beau.

"Just for the weekend."

"Gosh, Lynn, don't you think that's just a bit selfish? Hey, I'm a knight. Why don't I just drag some young lad off, and have my way with him?" Cass countered.

"Like he might object?" Lynn pointed out a likely candidate. "How about?"

"Too young!"

"And him?"

"Too fat."

"Picky, picky. Okay, how about the blond number?"

"Too pretty."

"Oh, my," Lynn said, her head swiveling around. "Goldilocks, I think this one's just right!"

"Which one?" Cass craned her head, but couldn't see who had Lynn so excited.

"There! Ten o'clock, just beyond the scarlet tent. The beard. Shorter than you, taller than me." There were a great many men with beards and a fair number fit the rest of Lynn's profile, but Cass followed the line of her gaze and found the one Lynn meant.

And had to confess, he was a fair piece of work. She tilted up her shades to get a better look. His hair was more silver than not, as was the short beard, and his features had the rugged stamp of someone who spent the bulk of his days outdoors. There was an air of strength and solidity about him as well, something Cass always admired in a man and all too rarely found.

"Not in garb," she commented. "Nobody I recognize."

"Me neither. But the word is the War's expecting better than five thousand people this year, so it stands to reason even us old-timers can't know everyone."

"I hate to say so, Lynn, but he doesn't have the look. I figure him for a local, up for a casual look-see."

"Or a history prof on holiday . . . Coo, though, he's spotted you."

"I doubt it's me he's after. You're the one with the décolletage."

"Don't be an idiot, Cass, maybe he's a leg man. Just turn around and *look*, what does it cost?"

Cass casually turned, fixing what she hoped would be a pleasant smile on her lips. Across the crowd their eyes locked. Some emotion in Cass convulsed, and she could feel her face go numb, her smile frozen in place. She trembled, quivered on edge—

"Cass!" Lynn snapped.

"What?"

Her friend spoke in a calm voice and a still, deliberate cadence that meant she was deadly serious. "Take your hand off your sword. Right now!"

Cass looked down and found herself staring stupidly at her half-drawn blade.

"The rules, Cass. You helped write 'em, remember? You draw steel, and you're out of here!"

Cass shoved the blade home and then stared at her hand, as though it had suddenly become some alien creature, independent of her will. "Thanks . . . " she started to say, and shook her head. "That guy, when our eyes met, it was like some memory . . . "

"I know. You were totally gone."

"Who *is* he? I wonder if I do know him, somehow?"

"Well, if he's your worry, forget about it. I can't see him anymore. Last time I try and find you a date."

"Look, do me a favor. I'm too wired to carry this." Cass quickly unbuckled her sword belt and refastened it around Lynn's waist.

"I hate these things," her friend protested.

"I know," Cass replied, "but how dashing you look. Now, where did that guy go? Maybe he ducked into a pavilion?"

She was already on the move.

"Cass!" Lynn called.

"Stay there a minute, I'll be right back!"

"*Cass!*" Lynn called again.

"Only a minute!" She did a quick pivot and ran a few steps backward while she explained, "If the guy's around, I want to know why he spooked me. I promise not to throw the first punch. Scout's honor!"

But when she cut around to the opposite side of the tent, she found only more tents and more people. Too many places to go, too many bods in the way. Hard as she looked, she couldn't see a sign of the man, and her instincts didn't suggest even the hint of a trail to follow. She stood in the shade of the scarlet pavilion, to get her bearings. She was ready to call it quits and go back to Lynn when a snatch of conversation from within the tent caught her ear, and she found her interest hooked like a trout on a fly.

" . . . don't look at me like that!" She heard a man's voice that hadn't quite broken at puberty. "I know this sounds crazy, but I spent six months in Edinburgh doing the research. The Glenowyn Grimoire is absolutely authentic. It's priceless, I tell you!"

He began pleading. "I've made all the preparation. I came up early, I snuck into the campground before anyone else arrived." His tone took on a veneer of pride. "Over the past week I've cast the preliminary invocations; I've placed the keys in the locks and turned all but the last. But to complete the summons and open the gate, I need a royal witness. And it must be tonight." No pride now, only urgency; the sales pitch wasn't going well.

"Don't you see, it's your answer. A crown no one can challenge. When they see what you've done—what *we've* done—they'll have to acknowledge the truth. That only you have the true legitimacy to be High King, and not for any stupid three-year term."

Cass had to make an effort to keep from laughing. The man was so serious with his playacting he'd lost his grip. But she

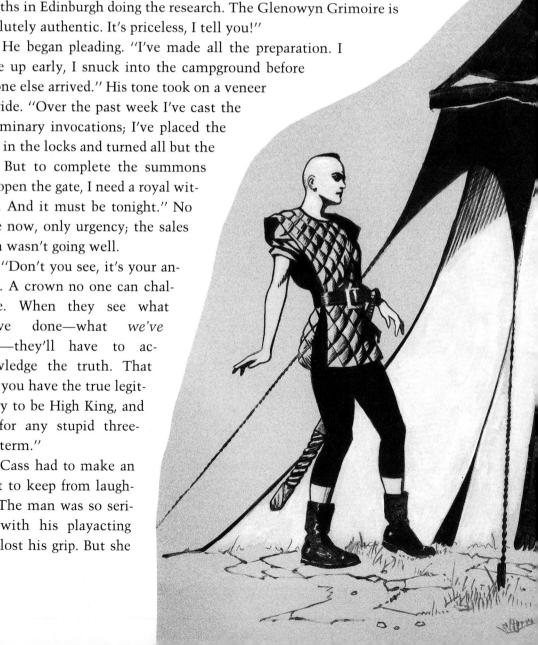

was likewise intrigued to discover just who the man was talking to, though she had a good idea. She edged closer to catch any response, but the voice was pitched too low to be heard over the hubbub of the camp.

"Hey, Dunreith!"

It was Lynn, with impeccable timing.

"You pulling a disappearing act as well?"

The flap of the tent was thrown back, catching Cass by surprise and making her jump. A gangly, cranelike figure appeared to loom over her like a telephone pole, his limbs too long for the torso that anchored them. His beard was as patchy as it was sparse, and his hair looked like it hadn't been washed in the week he'd said he'd been there. What Cass could see was all planes and hollows, mostly hidden beneath a cleric's long robe that she thought would be beastly uncomfortable in the midday heat. He wasn't sweating, though.

She didn't recognize him, but he did her, and his lip curled in a contemptuous sneer.

"You!" he crowed.

"Me?"

"You're not wanted here. Go away!"

She tried for a look past him, for a sight of the other person, but the young man stepped forward roughly to block her view. He was pushing for a fight, and Cass knew it was up to her to back down.

"Well, excuse me! Come, fair Mélisande, we'll leave this boy to his games."

But as she gathered up Lynn she offered a parting shot with a laugh. "Good luck tonight. But what will you do if by day's end, your patron is no longer Royal?"

⚜

Those words came back to her a few hours later, with the shadows stretching long across the field. Her body was one continuous ache from top to toe. Her lip was bleeding from a fresh hit, and she knew without looking that the rest of her was decorated with a scattering of bruises. Her only consolation was that Fieran didn't look much better. Over the course of the day, and through increasingly more demanding encounters, each of them had taken some heavy blows.

But they'd both survived, to finally face each other.

They were matched for height, but he'd added to his bulk since last year, pumped up by pumping iron. Designer body, Cass noted when they took the field, to go with designer clothes and home and job. Fieran lived his life as though it was a magazine spread. She'd heard it said that his garb and gear were custom-made, from some Hollywood design studio.

Of course, a day's hearty combat had done its damage and marred the sheer perfection of both man and armor. She knew he wouldn't like that, and wondered whether he'd use makeup to hide the marks or choose to display them like trophies.

She faced him in a half crouch, to make herself a smaller target but also because she was simply too damn tired to stand up straight. She'd never felt so exhausted, or so empty. The joy she'd felt in the morning's victories faded in the face of Fieran's obsession.

Moreover, the fatigue had cost her two key assets, her speed and her agility—and while Fieran was moving pretty slow himself, with his strength that wasn't a significant loss. All he had to do was stop her from tagging him with a fatal blow and continue to wear her down, waiting for the opening he needed.

She circled him in a delicate crab-footed sidestep, her rattan sword held in both hands while she warily eyed Fieran's *naginata*. Her busted lip had come from a blow with its butt ostensibly aimed at her shoulder (a legal blow) that had glanced off to hit her full in the face (not one bit legal). But she'd flinched fast enough to counter the force of the impact and immediately backpedaled out of range, waiting for the referee to call it. He was Fieran's man, and said nothing.

Fieran came for her with an overhead sweep of the spear. She blocked it momentarily with her sword, then ducked under the haft to let it slip by so she could come up with a countering lunge to his midriff. But Fieran used his momentum to bring the spear around to parry her attack, forcing her to disengage.

Only this time he came after her, another strike to the face that turned into a feint as he cracked the butt hard against her leg, right behind the padded plastic of her knee guard. The pain was excruciating and her first thought was that he'd broken a bone. She staggered, all thought of the combat cast aside, and in those moments of confusion, he delivered a pair of elegant touches to finish her off, within the rules.

Immediately, he turned away from her to face his pavilion and the cheers of his entourage, ignoring the bellowing from Cass's camp. It was George, charging onto the field like a bull for the matador.

"Foul!" he roared, echoed by the crowd. "Foul! Open your eyes, dammit, he went for her knee, he should be disqualified!"

Cass was yelling herself, putting aside the pain, furious that Fieran had used such an underhanded move, doubly furious that she had lost. She bellowed the King's name like a battle cry:

"Fieran!"

He turned at the sound as she put everything she had into a roundhouse baseball swing that cracked her rattan sword across his helmet like a bat. The shock was tremendous. Both sword and helmet shattered, pieces of wood and molded plastic flying everywhere. He staggered and actually fell, hand going reflexively to his face, a look of stark terror there that she was going to hit him again. She stood straddle-legged over him, lungs working like bellows, so possessed with rage that she was bouncing. No one watching had the slightest doubt that this battle had suddenly turned deadly serious.

George tackled her.

"Jesus Mary, Cass," he cried as they hit the ground and he literally buried her beneath his massive form, holding her in case she made a try to escape. "*Chill!* What the hell possessed you, woman, you damn near took his head off!"

"He damn near broke my leg!" she howled in reply. But she didn't struggle. The shock of George's intervention had broken the spell of the moment. She was still furious, but she was regaining control. Lynn rushed to her, pulled off Cass's knee guard, and expertly felt the battered joint for any significant damage.

People were running from all across the field—combatants and onlookers alike—forcing the Master of the Lists to shove his way roughly through the rapidly growing crowd in order to reach them. He was winded and visibly upset as he took position between Cass and Fieran, looking rapidly from one to the other, as though half expecting them both to leap up and start again.

"What the *hell*?" he said, echoing George's cry.

The referee leveled his baton at Cass.

"I cry you foul, Lady Siobhan," he charged formally, although his voice wasn't up to the task in strength or timbre, "and craven, for striking your opponent after the conclusion of the match, with intent to do him real harm!"

That brought George to his feet and he put himself right in the referee's face. "The hell you say! Didn't you hear me yelling? All of us, we saw it, Fieran fouled her first!" There was a grumble of agreement from the onlookers.

The Master of the Lists stated calmly, "I saw no foul."

"You calling me a liar? Fine, I say you're an ass-kissing buddy-boy of Fieran's, if you didn't see that foul!" George was quickly losing control.

The Master of the Lists explained patiently, "I'm not saying there was no foul, just that I didn't see it." He turned to the referee. "What happened here? Remember, you stand as a representative of all the Domains—an impartial, unbiased observer."

The man shrugged, trying to hide a smirk. "I guess Milady is a bit emotional at losing the match." He shot a glance at Fieran.

One of the crowd yelled, "Why's your nose so brown, Billy-boy?"

The day was turning ugly.

The Master of Lists pounded his ceremonial staff on the ground in a call for order. He turned to Fieran. "My lord, how say you to this charge?"

Fieran, breathing heavily, whether from the combat or from anger, blood streaming from his nose, answered, "There was no foul, intentional or otherwise. She slipped, I struck her fairly—which is more than you can say for her in return."

"Bullshit, you son of a bitch!"

George lunged for him, fist cocked. The Master of the Lists put himself between George and Fieran. Losing his composure, slipping out of character, he yelled, "Back off, Faraday! Has *everyone* here OD'd on testosterone? Are you nuts?

"I mean it, George, back off, or I'll file a formal complaint and bounce your raggedy ass off this field and out of the whole friggin' camp!" The seriousness of his threat stopped George in his tracks.

He turned back to Fieran, pulling the tattered cloak of his official duties around himself. "Now, I ask you, my lord Fieran, as Master of the Lists to a pledged knight, is what you said the truth: That you did not foully strike the Lady Siobhan, nor win this Champion's Combat by other than fair means? My lord, upon your word of honor?"

"He doesn't have one!" came another cry from the gathering crowd.

Fieran knelt down on one knee before the Master of the Lists and offered up his rattan sword. "Upon my word of honor, as a knight of this demesne, as a crowned King, and upon my sword, I do so swear." And he prettily kissed the blade.

Cass slowly pulled herself up from the ground, where Lynn had been nursing her bruised knee. Her throat hurt like hell from her war cry, and she rasped, "I, too, have something to swear." She moved to stand directly in front of Fieran, her eyes drilling into his. "I swear that I did indeed strike after the combat had been called, and so broke the rules of this engagement. *My* honor demands that I withdraw myself from this Champion's Combat. This is my word, the word of Cassandra Dunreith!" She reached around to pull her steel blade from the scabbard at Lynn's waist, and plunged it into the ground between them.

Fieran, pinned by her gaze, flinched.

It was a glum group that puttered around the campsite that evening. Dani and Stefan, Lynn and George all tried to break her mood, but Cass would have none of it. Chips and salsa were spread on the picnic table, but all she applied herself to was a bottle of red wine. Truth be told, George wasn't much better, and they traded stories about the Good Old Days, college, when life was less complex. It was hours later and full dark before Bosche returned, with news from the Council of the Four Kings.

"So what's the word, Bosche?" Cass called out half drunkenly from the beach chair where she sprawled, licking her wounds. "Am I scorned, cast out, banned for life?"

Bosche snorted. "You wish! No, it's a bit more complex than that." Everyone gathered closer to hear the outcome.

"Fieran is not as well liked as he thinks. The other three Kings and the regional secretaries were inclined to believe that he was lying, but as the Master of the Lists couldn't swear that he saw the foul, and as Cass had conceded the match, the crown stays with Fieran."

" 'Uneasy lies the head that wears a crown,' " Cass intoned in a deep, ominous voice. Her friends stared at her. "Oh, give up, guys, it's only Shakespeare! Don't worry, I wouldn't dirty my hands with that little shit."

"That's good, Cass," Bosche said, "because the Council made it very clear that while they're willing to look the other way on this one, you and George are not to so much as glance sideways at Fieran for the rest of the War."

"We wouldn't think of it!" they chimed in unison.

"But what about Fieran?" Lynn asked. "Tell me he got clean off?"

"No, they read him the riot act, about how the Society required other skills from the Kings than just whacking people with swords. If he can't get along with the members in his own kingdom, he'll be removed for the good of the Society."

"So after all this, he'll probably want to kiss and make up," George said disgustedly.

"That was recommended. And it was also suggested that Cass might want to change her allegiance to a different demesne after this weekend."

Everyone looked at Cass to see how she would take the news, as transferring to a different demesne would concede this personal battle, if not the war, to Fieran. Hands clasped behind her head, she was staring thoughtfully up at the sky. She shook herself and rasped, "A butt, a butt, my kingdom for a butt!"

Dani tossed over her pack and Stefan a lighter. Lynn said conversationally, "You don't have a kingdom, remember? You lost."

"She was robbed, Lynn!" George answered.

"Aren't we being a bit merciless?" Dani added.

"My point is, the legionnaires didn't shout, 'Hail the *conquered* hero,' did they?" Lynn stood up from the picnic bench and faced Cass. "You know I never pay much attention to this fighting stuff, Cass, but I'm still a pretty good judge of character. You can whup Fieran's ass with one hand tied behind your back when you're concentrating. You didn't, because you didn't want to win bad enough. Fieran would have sold his own mother for that crown. Am I right, or am I right?"

Cass stood, gingerly stretched, and stubbed her cigarette out on the ground. A shallow nod, a flick of her eyebrows, and she conceded. "Lynn, you're right. I just don't see the point of all this posturing anymore. The hell with it. I'm going to stretch my legs."

"They'll still be dancing up at the Barn," Dani suggested, but Cass shook her head.

"Not tonight, I'm not in the mood for that much company. I think I'll wander down to the stream."

"I'll come along," offered George.

"Go dance, Rags, I'll be fine."

"Don't forget what happened to that girl who was skinny-dipping a few years ago!" Dani said, with genuine concern.

"But since those guys were banned for life, even the Barbarian Horde has been somewhat civilized." Cass snapped off a mock salute. "And don't forget, the Lady Siobhan was once King's Champion, and should still command a little respect."

⚔

Roughly central in the campground was a man-made lake, circled by a one-lane access road posted the GREAT MIDDLE HIGHWAY on the western shore, and GREAT EASTERN HIGHWAY on the opposite. Farms bordered the campground on three sides, with an interstate marking its eastern boundary; the camp itself was mostly rolling fields broken by patches of woods. As you turned into the entrance, you could go right or left past the Troll Booth—Cass had gone left—to the two main camping areas. The place seemed crowded now, but Cass knew that by Saturday morning things would be a lot worse, the campground transformed into a fair-sized medieval tent town, the parking field jammed full of bikes, cars, vans, trucks, RVs, all abandoned for the weekend. The torches scattered here and there along the lakefront would form an almost unbroken line, and it would seem that nearly every square foot of land had a tent growing on it.

The popularity of the War was beginning to bother some in the Society, who feared things were getting out of hand, the event becoming too big to control properly. Cass was inclined to agree, but then she had always been a solitary sod, far more likely to keep to herself than share with others. Tonight, she knew, was a perfect example. Her friends had offered help, sympathy, comfort—whatever she demanded, they'd have cheerfully given—but she'd turned them away. Her misery hated company.

Headlights punched through the mist from behind her and a pickup growled past, pulling off the road at the Traditionalist camp, Society members who refused to use any modern tools during the War. No flashlights, no boom boxes, they wanted the medieval experience to be as true to life as possible.

Cass glanced at her watch. It was barely midnight, yet the field was far more quiet and still than she had ever remembered, even this early in the week. A lot of people approached the War like a convention, as the ultimate party experience where you *never* went to bed and the more carousing you did, and noise you made while doing it, the better. But tonight, even the infamous Tuchuks, that tribe of self-styled barbarians, were holding their peace.

She heard a faint splash echo across the water, followed by a few moments of chaos as a family of ducks took flight, quacking their annoyance at whatever had disturbed their sleep. She stood listening awhile, for any sign of what had startled them, then scooped up a couple of flat stones and sent them skidding across the surface of the lake, to break the silence herself.

On the face of it, the Council's proposal seemed eminently sensible. But it galled her—no, truly pissed her off—that the group she had worked so hard to establish, had given so much of her time and energy to, was now poised to cast her out. Time passed, life changed, and one generation gave way to the next. Cass spent nowhere near the time she used to devote to the Society and its business. That didn't mean that she enjoyed being put out to pasture like a tired old workhorse. Especially when it meant giving over to Fieran and his sort.

She'd always loved fantasy; telling stories to herself had been her way of easing the pain when she found herself alone and, she believed, exiled from home, abandoned in a strange country to live with family she barely knew. Of course she'd been told of the accident that had claimed her parents' lives, but the words hadn't really meant anything to her eight-year-old self. One day, the world had been a wonderful place; the next, all that was destroyed and she was sure she'd never be happy again.

In school, she'd wandered into theater, and discovered a knack for fencing. George was an early partner, and through him she'd met Lynn and the others, and through them, the Society. It was friendship that brought her here; friendship and fellowship, what gave this aspect of her life meaning.

Take away the one, she thought, *what reason remains for the other?*

The road led Cass into the woods where, on Sunday morning, two armies would come together in a wild-and-woolly mock battle, the last of the week's major engagements. This was the most fun, too; a warrior could be slain time and again yet always be resurrected to fight—and die—as often as he or she liked. The official duration of the combat was two hours, but Cass remembered a memorable summer when it seemed to go on all day, everyone was so juiced with adrenaline and having too much fun to stop. On the other hand, two years ago, the temperature had been in the nineties, infinitely worse for someone in armor, and she'd called it quits with her first "death." Once, she'd survived completely unscathed; another time, she'd been evacuated to the county hospital with a broken arm. She should be looking forward to it, Fieran or no, but she wasn't; the grim, anxious, edgy feeling she'd had ever since she arrived had returned with a vengeance, and she was getting tired of it. Whatever in herself that was determined to ruin her favorite weekend, one of too few now spent with old friends, she was equally determined to ignore, or drive away. And Fieran be damned!

A path led off the road into the forest, the exit marked by a small set of bleacher seats. Cass needed her flashlight to pick her way through the darkness, as the waxing moon couldn't penetrate the thick growth of trees. About fifty yards along the winding, and in places, *very* muddy track, she came upon a fast-flowing stream, dubbed by a Tolkien fan in the Society as the Lesser Greyflood. No one else was about, and the stream looked too inviting. Cass quickly hung her cloak and clothes on a tree branch, peeled off her sandals, and stepped gingerly over the high bank into the water.

Her breath caught in her throat. It was *freezing*, she wailed silently—and she plunged in. The violence of the current caught her by surprise. She should have expected it, given the amount of rain that had fallen recently, and she had to scramble to avoid being swept over the cataract just around the bend. The swimmable stretch was about fifty feet long. She began a steady crawl from one end to the other, letting the current pull her back before starting again. The combination of the cold water and the gentle exercise was working wonders on her tender knee. After ten laps, she sprawled in the shallows by the cataract; another ten, she decided, and she'd call it a night.

The stream's strong current massaged her sore body, gently pummeling all her aches and bruises. She cast herself adrift, let herself go to that place that lies between awake and dream, balancing delicately between equal parts of both. She found herself dancing, wild and free and alone on a heath-covered hilltop; the more the song demanded of her, the more she gave, with a joy as fierce as it was terrifying and a poignant intensity that gripped her soul. She had a sense of another presence, but she didn't try to look, she didn't really care, all that mattered was the music. A hand caught hers, a second joined the dance, his every move a perfect mirror of her own.

Then she came down too hard on her right foot in the dreaming, and triggered a sympathetic resonance in the flesh. Her leg spasmed, the pain from her knee made her cry out, and in that instant she lost her perch and fell into the current, and had to scramble awkwardly to catch hold of the bank before she was swept downstream over the falls.

As she dragged herself back she did a fast three-sixty, eyes coursing the shadows to reassure herself that whoever, whatever had shared her dream had no companion in reality. Then she made herself go all still, to give her ears a try. She dunked her head underwater to let the cold wash the cobwebs from her brain and thought just how stupid and New York neurotic she was acting. Then came up again, very fast, her body gone all tense as she held her breath—

—There *was* a tune on the breeze, making itself heard over the rushing water, a faint skirl from instruments that could be pipes or fiddles or perhaps whistles. She felt her pulse pick up to match the beat, and a hot flush spread beneath her skin to counter the chill of the stream.

A flash erupted from upstream, beyond the bend where she'd left her clothes, a strobe of pure, blinding white light that etched the trees in chiaroscuro silhouette, making them stark, abstract shapes without any depth. The radiance vanished as quickly as it had appeared, leaving her night-blind, with chaotic afterimages burned onto her retina.

No more music, Cass thought, while she waited for her eyes to adapt once more to the darkness.

Intrigued, she pulled herself silently along the bank, until she had a decent view of the clearing beyond. She dimly made out a gangly figure across the way, clad in what looked to be a monk's habit. While she watched, the cold water swirling around her belly, he threw off his robe to stand slim and naked in the faint, shadow-dappled moonlight. There was a dark patterning on his skin, a paint of some kind that formed intricate whorls, which covered him from top to toe. *Kicky makeup,* she thought with a nervous smile, *I couldn't have done better myself.*

He held out his hand, and a sword was passed from the shadows beneath the trees. In the same moment—*probably on cue,* Cass noted sourly—the waxing moon cleared the trees overhead and flooded the scene with light. Cass reflexively hugged the bank and hoped that whatever ceremony the young man had in mind wouldn't take too long. Since joining the Society, she'd been exposed to her share of esoteric religions and their practices, and had learned to take them more or less in stride. While she didn't want to disturb the ritual, she was also getting pretty damn cold. It wouldn't have bothered her so much when she was younger, but she didn't relish the thought of hauling herself out of the water buck-naked in front of strangers.

The young man began to chant, in a harsh, guttural tongue that Cass thought could have been Old German, or maybe bastardized Gaelic. He held the sword over-head, offering it up to the moon. With violence, he stabbed the ground with it, and used its point to describe a pentagram enclosed within its protective circle. Some-thing about the blade caught Cass's attention and she squinted in the uneven light, trying to see it more clearly.

The young man bent, placed a candle at each of the star's five points, and lit them. By the soft golden glow Cass saw him take his place at the center of the pentagram and reverse the sword, plunging its hilt into the soft ground, pinning the quillons with his feet, leaving the blade standing point upward. He began a litany: *"Abamo, Axir, Palco, Datt . . . "*

A voice answered, the body hidden from Cass's view, and she had to concen-trate in order to hear their words over the swift-flowing stream. Both voices contin-ued in unison:

> "From the north, east, south, and west,
> From the Land Beyond, and the Land Between,
> A host is summoned, transformed from shadow,
> Summoned in the name of a King twice-crowned,

Summoned to his side and honor-bound
To serve as knights to a true-born lord!"

"What's wrong," she heard from the trees, "why have you stopped?"

"I don't know," came the young man's jittery reply, his voice breaking. "I don't want to go on. This doesn't feel right."

Cass nodded agreement—she swore she could see the dissonant energy crackling through the air.

Who are these people, she wondered, *just what has the cat dragged in?* She threw her carefully schooled tolerance aside and thought, *This is not right.* Whatever was happening here she wanted no part of it. But how to get out of the water without drawing their attention?

"Why not? This is fantastic! Just think of the power you wield!"

"You don't understand . . . !" The celebrant's plea spiraled into a childish whine.

"No." That single word, rich with authority, brought the man's head up as if he'd been slapped. "I don't. You're not frightened, are you? We're here together; let's finish this."

The man tried to stand his ground; he stood as straight as he was able, as a measure of his defiance. But Cass knew he was beaten from the start, his body language made that plain.

"Crown," snapped the figure in the shadows, and Cass's mind screamed, *I know that voice!*

"Calls crown," responded the young man, in little more than a whisper, his stutter making the word barely comprehensible. And he held out his arms, embracing the sword.

Cass gasped, in surprise and wonderment, as the patterning on his body began to glow ever more brightly, until he cast his own shadows and she swore the fire would consume him.

Magnesium, she thought, *just a neat trick.*

But the hackles rose on the back of her neck and her breath caught in her throat.

"Forged in fire, cooled with blood—" Both voices wound together, invoking what Cass couldn't even imagine, the celebrant's voice dropping an octave, gaining the resonance and tone of a much older man.

"Nine times nine the goddess dance
is sung, and through the wood
the stag-king runs.
By this night's moon
the hunt's begun."

The woods were still as stone, the world touched with absolute silence, as if it were a bubble waiting to burst. Cass realized she was holding her breath, and for the first time in her life questioned the wisdom of being alone, at night, in the woods.

I don't want to be here, she hissed silently; *none of us should be here!*

The young man stood with bowed head and slumped shoulders, the blazing sigils etched on his skin. "By soul," he said, "I summon thee!"

To Cass, it was as though a star had come into being, right before her eyes. She'd never seen, never *imagined,* such an impossible radiance, at one and the same time both too terrible to be endured and too beautiful. The sane reaction—to save her sight—would have been to duck behind the earthen bank, but she was mesmerized by the scene beyond. Like the celebrants, she had to see it through to whatever end.

"By blood," the young man said, "I summon thee!"

And, impossibly, the intensity of the light doubled as the young man swept both hands up the sword and then into the air, throwing back his head and arching his body to its fullest extension. There were deep slashes in both palms, black blood flowing freely down his arms, spiraling through the blazing sigils. One symbol led into the other, and while Cass watched in growing horror—shaking her head from side to side in dumb denial of the ceremony—the paint on his body and the light it cast turned scarlet. The man was screaming, his voice filling the woods, and small wonder, because it seemed to Cass as though the awful radiance was actually burning its way through his body.

She was yelling herself now, all notion of hiding cast aside as she scrambled for her feet, determined to stop the ceremony and furious with herself for having waited too long.

"By life," she heard from within the circle, and knew she was too late.

"Stop!" she cried.

"I summon thee!"

And the young man threw himself forward, toward his blade.

The hairs crawled on the nape of Cass's neck and she was already clawing her way up the bank as a blinding explosion blasted the grove, hurling the young man out from his protective circle and Cass head over heels into the river. Perhaps that was what saved her sight, having her back to the circle as it exploded, casting a light so pure and absolute that every other aspect of reality was washed away.

She reeled, floundering and night-blind, trying to regain her balance in the swift-rushing thigh-deep water.

"The Riders," she heard, and assumed it was the boy, the words high-pitched with a stark and primal terror. *"The Riders!* The Gates of Knockma are flung wide, the Hunting Horn has sounded, and all the Wild Powers that were are loosed once more, to haunt the waking world! Hide from them, hide hide *hide* . . . !"

31

She sensed more than saw massive shapes gathering on the opposite bank, heard, unbelieving, metal armor rasping against leather cuirass, and horses breathing hard. She threw up her hands to protect herself as the horses wheeled, then charged toward her, fording the river, rushing past her, rushing *through* her, Cass hoping desperately not to be trampled. When the last horse was by she turned, face uncovered, toward the bank. There, horse and stag-helmed rider paused, silhouetted against the golden moon, to stare hard at her before thundering off.

She was ashore almost immediately, groping for her clothes. Fixating on the practical as her only source of sanity, she found her flashlight, stumbled about, searched for the celebrant, found him limp on the ground with eyes wide open and staring, far from consciousness. He was breathing, his pulse racing, but she got no reaction when she passed her hand in front of his eyes.

She checked the young man quickly for lacerations, burns, broken bones. There was nothing on him but smudged blue body paint. He should have been trampled; Cass was positive the riders had come this way. He should have been bleeding, wounded, dead; Cass had seen him slash his hands and fall on his sword, but there was nothing, nothing at all.

She stood and bellowed, "I know there was someone else here, dammit! He's hurt, and I don't know if I can lift him! Come give me a hand!" But all that answered her cry was the sound of trees rustling, water rushing in the stream—the typical sounds of a forest at night.

Muttering "bloody hell," she wrapped him in her cloak and gathered him up in a fireman's carry and hobbled for the road. She slipped in the mud, crying out as her knee twisted under her, kept going despite the pain; the skinny sonovabitch was heavier than he looked.

"Miserable, motherless excuse for a sodding, stupid, worthless, brainless sadsack nutter," she growled with each step as she made her way toward the road, setting up a cadence to take her mind off her own pain. "What the bloody hell were you playing at?"

She spotted an old Land Rover bouncing its way slowly down the muddy road and flagged it down with one arm, the other wrapped tightly around her unconscious burden to keep him upright. To her surprise, an older man, looking to be in his late forties, stepped out. He looked incredibly familiar, but in the dark her shell-shocked, addled wits couldn't place him.

"What's the problem?" he asked, in a Scots accent that reminded Cass of her aunt and uncle and warm milk to chase away the midnight bogeys. "The boy drink too much?"

Cass thought carefully how to answer. "I'm not altogether sure. I was taking a quiet swim, when this idiot shows up to perform some sort of ceremony. Not a big deal, given all the neopagans in this crowd. I settled down to wait so I wouldn't

33

disturb him. But then he performed a stunt that backfired with what I guess was a magnesium flare, and passed out. I couldn't in conscience leave the stupid sod lying in the mud, though I'd like to!" She realized she was babbling and fell uncomfortably silent.

The man gave her a sharp look, as if he knew that Cass had left out more than she was telling. But all he said to her was, "Right then. Let's get you both off to the infirmary. He may be unconscious, but you don't look too steady on your feet, either."

Cass thanked the luck that had brought her a competent adult instead of one of the Society's younger and more easily rattled members as she and the unconscious man were bundled into the back of the Rover and rushed to the medical tent at the head of the High Road. Under the bright electric lights of the examining room, Cass wasn't at all surprised to find the face of the boy she'd spatted with at the Champion's Combat.

The doctor on call was asleep, but the duty nurse immediately roused her. Their conclusion was the same as Cass's: the young man—little more than an overgrown boy—was suffering from deep shock. They quizzed her and she told them almost all of what she'd seen, but then looked puzzled when Cass said he'd cut his hands. There were no injuries now, his hands were unmarked, she must have been mistaken in the confusion of the moment. Even a cursory examination told them this was beyond their capabilities, so the doc put in a call for the county paramedics and an ambulance to the nearest hospital. Cass required nothing more than a brace to immobilize her strained knee and a loaned staff to help her walk.

"Well, this War's off to a fine start," she grumbled to her rescuer over a hot cup of sweet tea thoughtfully provided by the nurse.

"Not such a good one, is it, my lady Siobhan? That was a nasty whack you took today, and dragging that poor bastard from the woods wasn't a help."

Cass peered intently at the man over her Styrofoam cup and tried to chase the exhaustion from her brain as she sought to place him. He was of medium height but solidly built, with graying red hair and the ruddy complexion of someone who spent his time out of doors.

She gave a start and snapped wide awake. "You're the fellow that Lynn and I saw at the Champion's Combat."

She eyed him warily and wondered why this innocuous man put her so on edge. "We didn't take you for your typical Society type. We figured you for one of the locals dropping in for a look at the loonies."

"Local I'm not, though I am something of a medievalist." He chuckled at a private joke.

"So where are you from?"

"Oh, here and there. Edinburgh, mostly. And, o' course, the Highlands. I don't think you fought as well as you could have today." It was a deft change of subject, but Cass was too tired to continue the pursuit.

"You and the rest of the peanut gallery—sorry, I don't mean to sound so sharp, but everyone except me seems to know that. I guess I underestimated just how much Fieran wanted to win, and how ambivalent I've become to all this pomp and ceremony." She offered a rueful smile. "Maybe it's nature's way of telling me to trade in Lady Siobhan this year, and just stick with Cass Dunreith."

"Do what you will, Cassie, you'll still be a lady, and with more honor than most."

She was sure she was blushing and, to cover herself, said, "And your name?"

"Brian. Brian Griffin."

"Well, Brian Griffin. I left some stuff by the creek. Can you spare me the trudge and give me a lift back down there?"

⚜

Brian had pulled the Land Rover off the road and onto the path, and left the high beams on to light his way. They were more of a hindrance than a help. It was way past moonset, and in the chill before dawn, the wet earth yielded a ground fog that ebbed and swirled though the tree trunks. Cass huddled alone in the front seat. She sighed and made some random clucking noises, just to have something to hear. She switched to whistling tunelessly, wondering what was taking Brian so long, chiding herself for her nervousness, when she saw that by the illuminated dashboard clock he'd been gone all of six minutes.

Something flickered at the corner of her vision and she looked quickly around, searching the gray shadows with eyes and ears. A muted jangling noise echoed in the fog—a horse's bridle, armor rubbing armor? A spotlight was mounted on the door. All she had to do was roll down the window to switch it on. . . .

Cass fought her nervousness and did just that. She swung the beam in an arc as far as it would go. It didn't help, and for all its candlepower couldn't penetrate the dense fog. She wondered if she should get out of the car and look; things were getting a little too spooky for comfort. *What the hell was keeping Brian!* She pounded the horn, then yelped as a form materialized out of the fog right at her elbow.

"*You bastard,*" she yelled, "you scared the life out of me!"

Brian just looked at her curiously as he climbed into the car and tossed her things onto the backseat. Cass realized how rude she was being.

"I'm sorry," she said weakly, "but between the knee and an overactive imagination, I was pretty damn creeped out by the fog. I'm usually not quite as high-strung as this," she added sheepishly.

"Don't worry over it, Cass, it's been a long night," Brian said. "I'm sorry I took so long, but I thought I'd look around the clearing, try and piece together what that poor sod'd been up to." He stared out at the fog, deep in thought.

"And?" Cass prompted.

"You said there'd been an explosion?"

"That's what I remember. But I also remember the guy slicing open his hands on a sword, so who can say for sure?"

"I didn't find a thing."

"No sign of the blast, you mean?"

"Aye. No sword either; no robe, no circle, not one thing."

"Are you sure that you were in the right clearing?"

"Fairly certain. One thing I did find—the ground was all churned up. If I didn't know better, I'd say a troop of horse had charged out of that river." Even by the dim glow of the dashboard lights, Brian's gaze was piercing. "Now tell me—why are you so upset? You don't look the kind to let foolish lads scare you."

Cass laughed hollowly. "I don't. So please don't laugh when I say I thought I was seeing things in the fog, except that every time I looked straight at whatever it was, there was nothing, nothing but that damn fog. . . . But hell, I'm a writer. No one's ever accused me of having an *under*active imagination."

"Phantasms don't leave hoofprints. If I didn't want an answer, I would not have asked you the question. What did you see?"

Cass sighed, and let her head loll back against the headrest. "Horses are banned from the campground. There's a stable nearby that we have access to, but after a nasty mishap it was judged too dangerous to bring them into the campground proper, especially with all the children running about."

"And?"

"Right after the explosion, right after that lunatic cut his hands and splattered blood on the ground, I saw armed men on horseback. Swords, armor, helmets, the works. They forded the creek and went into the woods."

"So who would flout the rules, and bring in armed riders?" It was a serious question, and she was grateful that he took her statement at face value.

"The same person who came back to the clearing to remove all the evidence. The same person who would cheat to win the Champion's Combat. A person for whom this War's the reality, and the rest of the year the fantasy. The person whose voice I'm certain I heard in the clearing, answering the celebrant. Fieran."

Her hair is long again, down past her knees, and she is running, stumbling, gasping through a dark wood, the blood pounding in her ears. Her long scarlet linen gown

snags on brambles and tears, and another scratch is added to the growing red lat-
ticework on her arms, hands, and face. Something slips down over her eyes and
blinds her. She grabs the white flowered wreath, and throws it hard away. Queen
of the May, Queen for just one day . . .

There are pursuers, but she can't hear them, can't see them, can only sense
them. Like ghosts slipping through shadow, they make no noise. Their leader, stag-
helmed, silhouetted against the full moon, sounds his hunter's horn, the echoes
ferreting out all the secrets of the dark forest. She seeks refuge in the gnarled
branches of a grandfather oak, kicking free of her sandals to scramble up its twisted
branches. Her damned long hair is caught, but the more she struggles to free herself,
the more tangled she becomes, until looking up, she sees that the glistening white
berries and twining green vines of the mistletoe that wind through the old oak's
branches are now winding through her dark hair, down her white arms, binding
her to the tree. She is caught, bound, helpless, the dogs baying, horse and riders
both panting for her blood, a wild hunt. She can smell the rank sweat of fear rising
from her skin, because now she truly knows that she is the hunted. . . .

⚕

Cass staggered from her tent the next morning (just a few hours, really, since Brian had returned her to her campsite) with a pounding headache and the surreal feeling of displacement that's the bitter aftertaste of a nightmare. She was damned if she would tell this one to any of her friends. Her imagination was too vivid, she'd read too many books. Last night was a doozy, was all.

George, bless him, was an early riser, and had a hot mug of strong coffee ready to jam in her hand. He stood behind her, patiently rubbing the knots from her neck as she bubbled and stewed her way through yesterday's events, not asking questions. This, Cass thought, is what made George her dearest friend. He was the only one who didn't take her bitching seriously; the only one who could make the anger go away.

Cass was just beginning to feel vaguely human when two fresh-scrubbed, pink-cheeked state troopers pulled up at the campsite, to ask for her version of the previous night's events. They thought it "best to return to the site of the incident" (*Why*, wondered Cass, *do they always have to speak jargon?*) "to best understand the order of the proceedings." After bumping down the track in the squad car and hobbling to the creek, she found things as Brian had described them the night before: there was no sign of the pentagram or the man's clothes, and the wet ground had indeed been trampled to a sodden mess.

The troopers were good, if hard to distinguish from each other, and Cass found herself making mental notes for a future story. Similar content, she decided, but a totally different form from the New York cops she'd seen in action.

When they asked, she pointed out her position just above the cataract and walked them through the ritual as she'd seen it from her vantage point. She slipped on a mossy stone and almost took another header into the stream, but one of the troopers had reflexes to match his hero's good looks and caught her before she got more than a foot wet. Even so, it was like stepping into ice water and Cass shook her head in amazement at how long she'd stuck it out the night before.

The questions were casual, the mood surprisingly relaxed, and Cass thought the two men were being remarkably patient. She herself would have been hard put to keep a straight face when presented with a tale of arcane rituals filled with blood, swords, fire, and naked young men. She stopped short of mentioning the horsemen or her suspicions about Fieran's involvement. Enough time for that later, if it proved necessary; in the meanwhile, she wanted first dibs.

The air was steamy under the forest canopy, and as Cass scanned the branches overhead she marveled at how she'd managed to see any moonlight at all. She'd brought a couple of bottles of water in her pack and offered one to the troopers.

The officer broke the seal and took a swallow, before handing the bottle off to his partner.

"Any notion who the boy is?" Cass wondered aloud.

The trooper smiled. "We were just about to ask you."

She shrugged. "Never seen him before yesterday."

"Yesterday? Not last night?"

She nodded. "He shooed me away from his tent during the Champion's Combat. That's where I first heard talk about this ritual."

"There was someone else involved?"

"I heard a voice, I didn't see a face. Not then, or last night."

"This ceremony, it took two people to perform?"

"Evidently. But I didn't see anyone else."

"You use drugs, Ms. Dunreith?"

She wasn't thinking, her mouth engaged before her brain could yell its warning.

"Lately, or ever?" she replied lightly.

Too late, she realized it was a serious question, and they'd taken her words as a serious reply.

"No," she said simply. "Why? Was he on something?"

"Do you believe in all this stuff? The ritual, I mean, the 'magic'?"

"If you're asking my religion, I'm Scots Presbyterian, about as unmystical as you can get," was what she said. What she thought, even as she spoke, was of a clearing filled with sanguine silver light. What she heard was a sound like music, and she made the mistake of responding.

39

"Something the matter?" asked the trooper, when she turned away from him, her face becoming taut with wary concentration.

"I thought . . . " she breathed, "I heard . . . "

Then she shook her head violently, as though to deny the moment and banish it from her awareness.

"It was nothing," she told the troopers.

"Pretty strong reaction for 'nothing.' "

"What are you saying happened here?" she demanded.

"We're not saying anything, miss," said the other trooper, who'd been quietly but thoroughly going over the scene while his partner did the talking. "You're the one who told us, remember?" Then he smiled, but his gaze never left Cass's face.

"We're done here, Gene," he said. "Give you a lift, miss?" he offered.

"I'll walk, thank you."

They started out of the clearing, but after a couple of steps, Gene—the better-looking of the two, the one who'd been handling most of the interrogation—stopped and looked back at Cass, as though touched by an afterthought. "You're sure that's everything, Ms. Dunreith? Nothing else you'd care to tell us?"

"Such as?"

"It's a pretty fantastic story, you've got to admit."

"It was a pretty fantastic night."

"We'll check on everything you've told us, miss," said Gene's partner. "Hopefully, when the victim recovers consciousness, his story will corroborate yours."

"Is that likely?"

"Corroboration?"

"His recovering consciousness. The doc here said he looked pretty bad when I brought him in."

Gene touched the brim of his hat. "We'll be in touch."

Back at her tent, Cass shucked the jeans and T-shirt she'd worn for the troopers' benefit with hard and angry gestures.

"Dammit," she snarled as she nearly tore a fingernail fumbling at the waist button. "Damn *them!*"

Someway, somehow, they thought *she* was responsible.

"This is the end," she raged, "the last straw. I've had it, I'm done, I'm fucking *gone!*"

She grabbed for her duffel and cast about for the first clothes at hand to stuff inside, with such violence that she twisted her knee. And then stopped, to give way to the pain.

"Yeah, right," she said mockingly, continuing her solo conversation. "Like they aren't waiting for me to do precisely that. I mean, look at it from their perspective; assuming foul play, who else they got as a suspect?"

Fieran, she thought brightly.

"After yesterday." She shook her head. "With all the history between us, I probably could have caught him *holding* that damned sword and nobody'd believe it. *Shit!*"

There was nothing she could do about the situation, and so thrust it aside. Instead, she grabbed for a light cotton tunic and sandals—her bruised and bandaged knee, she decided sourly, a wholly unattractive accent, and then grinned at the notion of passing it off (quite legitimately) as a war wound.

She gathered up her cameras and equipment bag and gimped off to shoot the camp. For the better part of the morning, she wandered the roads and paths, grabbing photos of whatever took her fancy: a kitten playing in someone's armor, peeking out from a helmet; young kids in medieval garb hawking the first edition of the camp newsletter; wild juxtapositions in costuming, such as the full-blown Disney princess wearing Ray-Bans and bopping to her Walkman.

Cass had always loved the riot of color that was the War. Good as her imagination was, she could never have come up with the infinite variations she saw on the medieval theme. A juggler, a blacksmith, a King, the numbers and variety of people seemed endless. For some, the point was to re-create the medieval experience as realistically as possible, for others, to fulfill their own fantasy. By the time she took a break, somewhere near noon, she'd cleared four full rolls of film and was beginning to doubt she had enough to last the War.

Coke in hand—bought from the camp store attached to the Barn—she stepped inside out of the sun, taking a moment to luxuriate in the shade before moving down the row of tables set up by merchants to hawk their wares. She saw jewelers and booksellers, potters, costumers, and swordsmiths. Just a few of the latter were actually worth the name. Cass hefted a claymore broadsword almost as tall as she was, made admiring noises, and looked at a Japanese *katana* at the next table so cheaply constructed that the blade had been warped into a shallow S-curve. The dealer was asking forty-five dollars, but Cass demurred; he called it a steal and she agreed, though probably for different reasons.

She bowed out of one conversation after another on yesterday's combat, and a host of annoying questions about what had happened during the night. To Cass, both subjects were under interdict; both events only served to remind her what an irritating mess her life had become. She ducked out the back entrance that led from the cool dark of the Barn to the hot June sunshine beating down on a row of colorful tents, for those craftspeople with enough of a reputation to warrant the additional space. Cass knew most of them by name, coming up with them, as it were, through the ranks of the Society. Here one could find real works of art, done by Society members whose craft wasn't just a hobby, but a full-time vocation. Cass stepped in to admire the jewelry of one longtime friend who showed in some of the best galleries on the West Coast, but wasn't quite tempted to make a major investment. As Cass emerged, hand shielding her eyes, sun-dazzled, she heard a familiar voice.

"Annie!" she cried, yelping in delighted surprise as the shorter, stouter woman gathered her up and whirled her around, hugging her fiercely, in a greeting that was returned in full measure.

"You look pretty fair, for damaged goods," Anne Harding said.

"Dumb luck, I guess, considering all that's happened lately."

"Yeah, I heard. Quite a night."

"And then some. Have you put on weight?"

"Why is it the people who notice that the most are the ones who never do, even though they eat like horses?"

"That isn't fair. I starve as much as you!"

"My point exactly. I get fat." They'd known each other since college and, of course, Anne had never been anything less than plump, no matter how hard she'd tried—exercise, diet, for her nothing worked. "But this year," she told Cass as she led the way inside her tent, "I get my revenge."

"Is that my cue to scram? Very nice place, very spacious," she added, looking at the Bedouin-style layout. "It looks sinfully comfortable." Anne's grin told Cass it was. "What's that?" she asked as Anne pulled a box into view.

"Gift. Enticement. Maybe a sale. For you, dear child, a change of character. What d'you think?"

"Wow," was all Cass could say at first. Anne was holding a coif made of light silver chain mail that covered the face as well as the rest of the head like a veil, with a line of glass rubies stitched up the center of the forehead from the bridge of the nose over the crown of the head and down the back. The eye slits as well were outlined in gems that glittered in barbaric splendor, even in the shadowed interior of Anne's tent. In the sun or especially the evening torchlight, Cass knew their effect would be magnificent.

"There's more," Anne said, and pulled an entire costume into view. There was a mail bra and G-string bellyband with a pattern of gems set right on the crotch that went over a pair of gauze trousers, plus an assortment of baubles and bangles to be

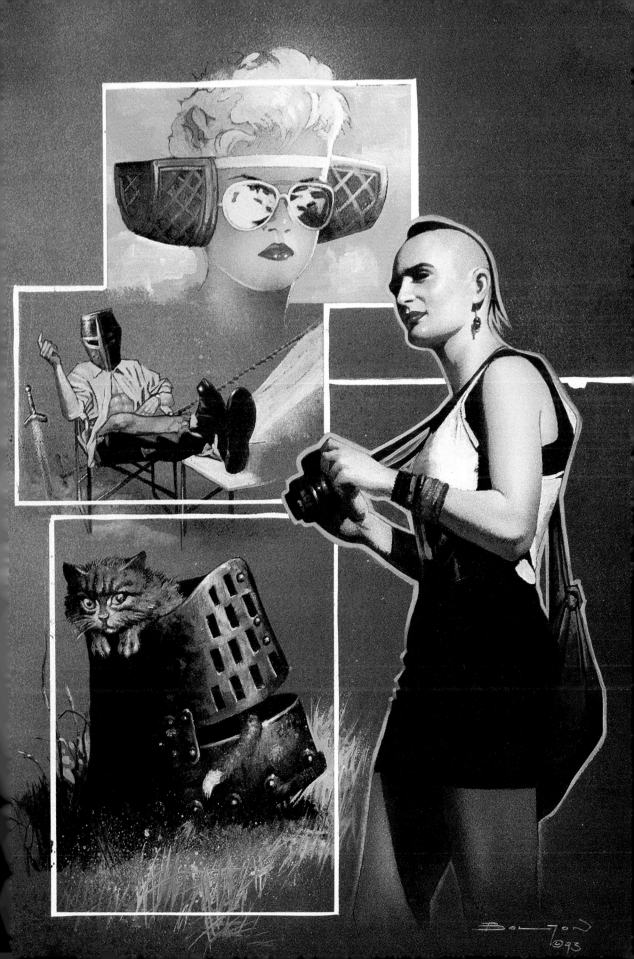

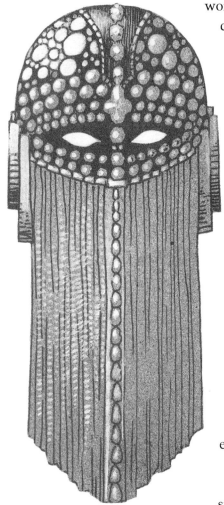

worn as accessories. Last, as protection from sun, wind, cold, or prying eyes, Anne presented a gorgeous white linen hooded caftan.

Cass slumped against a pile of plush pillows and frowned at her friend. "Annie, when I asked you to make me a costume, I was expecting something a little more . . . " She groped for a polite word.

"*Macha?* Butch? Sword-slinging?"

"Gimme a break."

"Part of your problem, kiddo, is that you take this mess too damn seriously. Loosen up, rattle the chains a little, shake the cage. Just 'cause those clods are used to you playing Lady Siobhan the Warrior Maiden doesn't mean you're stuck with the role. Try something new for a change, might do you good."

"Granted—but this?"

Anne handed her a wineskin (for courage, she told Cass) and went on to say, "Indulge me. I put a lot of work into it. At least, try the outfit on, let me give you the full treatment. If you can't stand yourself when I'm done, fine, I'll find another buyer. Fair enough?"

"You're making me feel guilty as hell."

"Serves you effing right for being such a spoil-sport. Do we have a deal?"

Cass sampled the wine and nodded, certain this was a decision she was going to regret.

An hour later, as Anne smoothed the last touches of makeup around her eyes and then lowered the headdress into place, she was nowhere near so sure. She didn't recognize the woman in the full-length mirror. The body was tanned and fit, without a spare ounce of fat; her breasts were small, although they looked fine, but her legs were damn near perfect, long and smooth and powerful. The gauze silk trousers showed them to good advantage, tying at hips and ankles, leaving the outside of the legs open. There was a jewel for the navel, anklets, armlets, bracelets, chain-mail sheathes fastened at the wrist that fitted over Cass's fingers and covered the backs of her hands, a gossamer skullcap to keep her hair from poking through the links on her head ("You were supposed to have long hair," Anne fumed. "Whatever possessed you to cut it off?" Cass's retort: "Just rattling the chains, babe, no one told me you were casting Scheherazade!")

Now that all was said and done, however, both women had to admit the effect was breathtaking.

"I'll need the caftan," Cass told Anne, "and probably a set of brass knuckles."

"You'll do fine."

"Where's that wineskin? I'm not leaving without another drink."

"Worth the effort, don't'cha think?"

Cass giggled, then choked as some wine went down the wrong way. "Jesus, Annie, if the people I work with in New York could see me now . . ."

"You ever consider, *chica*, that you might be too tough for your own good?"

Anne's tone was light and inconsequential but the question wasn't, and Cass answered in kind. "I am what I am, Annie."

"You happy with that?"

"I wouldn't be anything without it. Wish me luck."

"Luck. I'll take a check."

"Keep my cameras as security till I get back."

⚜

Cass knew it was late, but the sun was still well above the tree line, too hot in the open to wear the caftan for any length of time, and she was nervous enough not to want to take it off. She decided to take another stroll through the Barn. The crowd had grown. She heard a murmur that the attendance was already past a thousand cars, well over three thousand people.

She made sure to pass by merchants she'd visited earlier, but to her mingled amazement and delight, no one recognized her. Near the door, one young bravo sidled up to her, snaked his arm about her waist, and pulled her close to whisper rudely inventive suggestions in her ear. Lady Siobhan, approached thus, would have issued a challenge, but Cass merely spun out of his grasp and refused with an exaggerated curtsy that left him openmouthed and flabbergasted.

Cass gathered her caftan around her and started for the Rune Field and the lake road beyond, taking the long way back to her tent, grinning in anticipation of her friends' reaction to her new finery. New costume, new persona, and this one without a sword. Perhaps this was just the thing to shake off the bad karma that seemed to follow the Lady Siobhan, and the debacle that was yesterday's Champion's Combat. *What persona*, she wondered, *would go with this costume? Someone a bit naughty, probably proud, but certainly with a sense of humor. Perhaps Annie's right, and this is just the thing for my lovelorn, overworked self.*

She was in the woods once more, taking a shortcut, skirting the edge of the field. She hadn't passed anyone along the road, which was strange because a hot afternoon like this would ordinarily send scores of people down to the river for a

45

refreshing dip. It was a lot harder to see than she expected, too. The trees seemed to block out considerable sunlight. Cass quickened her pace. The grove wasn't friendly anymore, and she wanted to be out of it as soon as possible.

Right by the bleacher seats was the turnoff to the swimming hole. The still-wet ground was well churned by all the traffic it had seen since last night's adventure. Were those hoofprints mixed in with the tire tracks? She shivered, and thought it was curious that she was cold.

She looked back toward the woods. She'd heard a horse snort—which, she reassured herself, was patently impossible since none were allowed inside the campgrounds. *There,* she thought, *the chink of a bridle, a horse stamping. This is nuts!* She was still telling herself that when the rider came into sight, posed at the edge of the woods, looking toward her. Waiting.

His mount was a Thoroughbred charger, seventeen hands tall at the shoulder—bigger than she was—and the rider was built to fit, broad-shouldered and clad in well-forged black steel-and-leather armor. A shield was slung off one side of his saddle back, a sword at his hip, and Cass could see the handle of a huge war ax hooked over the pommel. The equipage was magnificent; it looked real, too, no costume prop like so much for sale in the Barn. His visor was down to hide his features; and both tunic and shield were blank—he bore no heraldic devices, the mark of an unaligned knight, a dangerous man.

Cass cursed the luck that caught her dressed as such a defenseless persona. Lady Siobhan, with her own armor and sword, wouldn't look like such easy pickings to a predator such as this. Lady Siobhan, most likely, would be foolish enough to fight. The rider was a hundred yards away, the sunlit boundary of the copse less than half that in the other direction, yet Cass didn't even try for the clearing. She sensed that was what he wanted, what he was waiting for. All her instincts screamed to her that the moment she made that move, he'd ride her down.

She hitched up the caftan and broke for the woods, praying her knee would hold, staying on the path for speed but ducking in and out of the trees along the way, choosing the smallest spaces, making herself as difficult a target as she could. The warrior had indeed spurred his mount into a gallop with her first step; she could hear him crashing through the woods behind her, trying to cut her off from the stream. He knew the terrain.

The horse was like a battering ram, the undergrowth and rough footing not slowing him down in the slightest. She dodged back toward the trail, giving the rider a clear shot at her, pausing a moment to slip her right arm from its sleeve before once more picking up her pace. Timing would be everything; a mistake, she was sure, would get her trampled or cut to pieces.

She was at the riverbank when another warrior materialized from the shadows, almost on top of her, so impossibly close she fancied she could feel his mount's steaming breath on her back when she pivoted, sweeping the billowing caftan off her shoulders and around into the animal's face. Startled and blinded, it tried to stop, rear, shy away, all at the same time and in the same motion, from a full galloping charge. Instead, the horse fell, brutally hard, pitching the rider from his seat.

Cass was already on her way back to the road—but she hadn't taken more than a few steps when she was blindsided with the shoulder of another gigantic mount. The collision sent her flying through the air into the middle of the river. The impact drove the air from her lungs and left her stunned; by the time she reached the surface, she was half-drowned, gasping desperately for air.

She was almost into the rapids, and for a fleeting instant she hoped this might be the means of her escape, but she came to her senses and grabbed the offered pike haft. Rough hands scooped her up and she was dragged ashore, to be dumped at the feet of the man she had unhorsed.

She didn't move, painfully aware of teeth chattering as much from fear as cold, wondering what was going to happen next and hoping it wouldn't hurt much. She thought of screaming for help and realized at the same instant that anyone who heard was in as much trouble as she. Her characters found themselves in situations like this all the time. They were heroes, this was their stock in trade. They always seemed able to cope, so Cass told herself to do the same. Then she laughed. This was silly, too fucking insane, it was one of her stories come to life.

Somebody grabbed her coif and yanked her head up; she cried out, but the sound that emerged was more like a snarl. The rider she had unhorsed had his helm off and blade drawn; the look on his face told Cass he intended to use it. He spoke in a guttural tongue that was like nothing she'd ever heard, yet seemed strangely familiar, and her headdress was yanked off and cast aside. To her surprise, he smiled—he saw something in her features he liked—and the warriors behind her stood her on her feet.

Close up, he was as impressive as what she'd seen of him on his horse, a head taller and so big that two of her could have fit inside his armor with room to spare. His thick hair, tied back with a thong, was black as night, while his eyes were so pale the iris seemed almost white; he was clean-shaven, lines of age and strain and humor etched deep into his face. He was as old and cruel as time, with the same inexorable power of the seasons. And there was an aura of command about him that even Cass found herself responding to.

With a fearsome cry, he swept his sword up and down toward her head with all his strength. There was no time to react, and so she didn't. Once, in a long-ago college acting class, she'd been stretched out on the floor, relaxing, when some toad decided to scare her by jumping into the air above her, making like he'd land on her face. At the last instant he'd split his feet apart to miss, bracketing her head by a fraction of an inch. She hadn't blinked an eye. She'd known instinctively that it was

either a bluff or she was dead and so there was no point in worrying either way. He'd been suitably impressed, and she made sure never to work with him again. This was much the same.

The rider stopped the blade with its edge touching her forehead; she felt a damp trickle between her eyes. He'd drawn blood. He scowled. Obviously that hadn't been part of the program, he wasn't such hot stuff as he'd thought, and she answered with a cold smile.

"Mharyon," cried one of the others, "she bleeds! You cut her!"

"Them's the breaks," Cass muttered, and only then did she realize that although the sounds remained harsh and guttural, like the backwoods Scots Gaelic she'd grown up with, she could understand what the men were saying. It must have been her fear that made the language sound so alien.

The leader—Mharyon—rubbed a thumb roughly across the cut before touching it to his lips and nodding. Before he could speak, one of his men pushed forward, black helm held under his arm, his red hair done with a warrior's braids. From his armor Cass knew that he was the one who had chased her down.

"Mharyon! I saw her first. I claim her as mine!"

Mharyon held her eyes and, without turning, replied, "I do not think she is mine to give."

"She is a vassal of this King who called us here. I want her company. It is my right."

"Shut up, Finn," Mharyon said, and struck him across his cheek. "As I thought, brethren," he announced, his voice booming through the glade, "she is of the Blood. We are well met, Lady." And he made a shallow bow.

"Who are you?" she demanded, cursing inwardly at the quaver in her voice.

"Riders of the Shadows, Riders of the Storm. You must know us, Lady."

"Quit the playacting. I'm not amused. You're breaking every rule of the War— not to mention the goddamned *law*—using edged weapons and drawing blood. I'll report you!" She stopped, fuming at the hollow words, wishing for her own sword.

"I am sorry, Lady. We are here at a King's command, and our arms for this short time are pledged to him. It is his bidding we must do."

Something clicked at the back of Cass's brain, but she spluttered, "Bullshit."

Cass could see the vulgarity hurt him. His eyes flicked over her bedraggled finery, and he spoke softly so just she would hear, "I can see that you were ill raised, *Lady*, and so perhaps do not know the ties of Blood." Louder, for the benefit of his men, he proclaimed, "Thou alone art free to walk thy road in peace, thou art kin, this affair hath naught to do with thee. Our apologies for the rudeness of *our* greeting, 'twas born of ignorance. We fare thee well, Lady." He and his men remounted. He wheeled his charger around, the animal rearing up on its hind legs and bugling, and Cass reeled as what seemed to be scores of giant men on larger horses thundered around—and, it seemed sometimes, *through*—her, following Mharyon into the woods, where they were almost immediately lost from sight and sound.

She stood alone for a moment, staring about in wonderment, absently picking her coif out of the churned mud on the bank, thinking how mad Annie would be with her. Then her eyes rolled up in her head and she pitched sideways into the water.

⚜

She stands within an ancient stone circle, high upon a tor. She can hear waves crashing below, smell the sea. The night is dark, no moon, just brilliant starlight, and she turns full circle to get her bearing. She turns again, and again, and finds herself sky-clad, spinning in circles, dancing in spirals, walking the labyrinth and laughing for the joy to be home.

The stars are rent with silver. Cass stops, heart pounding, panting. Turns slowly to see Mharyon, blade drawn, standing within the circle. His men stand sentinel, grim warriors strangely helmed, each between a standing stone.

"Lady!" Mharyon calls. "I ask: Who are you?"

"I do not know," Cass answers.

"What blood is in your veins?"

"My own!"

"Are you lost, then?" He mocks her. "I doubt it, as you have found this sacred place. (And the thought flares unspoken, This is *my* place, what right have you to face me here?)

He asks, "What say we play, and try and guess your name?" His sword flares with white-hot light as with a two-handed cut he slashes her naked belly. She doubles over, clutching herself, aghast with shock and hoping that there will be no pain.

"Who are you?" he demands.

"I don't know!" she replies, but rises, now clad in her favorite jeans and leather jacket.

"Who are you?" Mharyon demands, "Who sent you here?" He dances forward, strikes again.

"I don't know!" she replies, now in sweater and skirt, her eight-year-old self.

"Who are you?" he cries, and slashes again (but she sees that the effort is costing him).

"I tell you I don't know!" she whispers, and looks out at a world washed with gold, looks down at her obsidian skin.

"Lady! What are you?" he cries (is that fear in his voice?), and hoists his sword, preparing for another stroke.

"Enough!" she cries, and meets his sword with hers in a clash that shakes the stones. "I am Cassandra Dunreith, and that, Old One, is all you need to know!"

Heat blossoms within her, burns away doubt, and she throws back her head and laughs. Her back grows warm with the heat of the rising sun. Flame bathes the hilltop, washing all away, except Cass, and her crystal-edged sword.

🜁

The first thing she was aware of was her whole body aching. She stirred a little, vaguely conscious of comfortable softness beneath her and the tangle of a T-shirt close about her body, and concluded it was a proper bed and not the riverbank. She discovered that, bad as things felt, movement made them infinitely worse. She heard a voice rumbling in a familiar brogue, and her eyes snapped open, fixing on a very Scots face.

"Brian," she called, thinking she was shouting, unaware that her whisper was so soft it wouldn't have been heard had he not been sitting at her bedside. The air was stuffy and warm, the curtains above her tightly drawn, so she concluded it was day. But which one? How long had she been out? She asked, and after giving her a sip of water for her dry throat and chapped lips, he told her the afternoon had mostly given way to twilight.

"Make a helluva comic book."

She sighed. "I must've been swept through the rapids. Shouldn't I be in hospital or something?"

"If you remember that, I doubt there's any serious head injury, concussion or the like. That's what I was most worried about. As for the rest of you, it's all cosmetic. You'll be some very pretty colors for at least a week. Like a rainbow."

"Wonderful."

"It could have been much worse."

"This your tent?" She looked around, noting its sparse but comfortable layout, like something out of a classic Abercrombie & Fitch catalog. Camp cot, folding table and two chairs, Coleman lantern for light, a trunk for clothing and gear . . . *As well prepared as an old campaigner,* she thought.

"After I found you, I took you back to your campsite, but your friends weren't about. I've some medical training I picked up during the war, and while you didn't look like you needed to be in hospital, I thought it best to have you where someone could keep an eye on you."

Cass smiled weakly. "Do you always appear in the nick of time to rescue damsels in distress?"

Brian answered in a more serious tone. "I thought there might be more to learn from that spot by the river. What happened to that young man remains unfinished business. But enough of this. Hungry?"

"Wouldn't mind." Brian busied himself for a few minutes outside the tent and returned with a bowl of steaming porridge.

"It's summer," Cass protested when she saw him.

"It's good for you. And it's best to stick with soft foods for the start, till you're more sure of your stomach. Try a bit, Cassie; after that, I'll not force you." She did, and was lost to the taste of cinnamon, brown sugar, and cream—as both had known she would be. When she sagged back against the pillows, the bowl was clean.

"So tell me, Brian, what the hell's going on here?" She had thought she'd meant the question as a joke, but when Brian didn't respond—and his silence lengthened—she realized he was taking it seriously. "Brian, *is* something going on? Tell me."

"What do you think?" he asked gently.

Cass spoke hesitantly, and kept one eye on Brian to gauge his reaction. "I think I was chased through the woods and thrown into the water by a band of armed knights on horseback. I think they have something to do with what happened last night at the stream. And I'm afraid that more people are going to get hurt."

"The young man whom you saw last night, at the stream, it appears he thought he was casting a spell."

"I told the police that. They weren't impressed. They think I'm responsible."

"Hardly a revelation. To them this War and the thousands of people that come to it are a nuisance, relics from the sixties or computer hacks on holiday. They don't give what goes on here much weight. And, with what's happening in the outside world, I can't say I blame them."

"For most of us, this is a giant playground, a chance to play dress up, a chance to be kids again. Be rowdy, get physical, in ways we don't allow ourselves in the mundane world. Don't get me wrong, we take what we do seriously. There's a lot of passion here, care, and love. But ultimately, for me at least, it's just a game.

"Brian, what the police don't realize is that to some people *this* is what's real, the nine-to-five world just a shadow. If they're casting a spell, they mean something by it. If they're wielding steel, it has an edge that can cut. If they're fighting a war, they mean to win." Almost without knowing it, Cass rubbed the cut on her head.

Brian looked down at her. "Fieran."

"That isn't his name, of course. We all assume personas when we join the Society, labels for the roles we play. Philip becomes King Fieran, Cass the Lady Siobhan. I heard he works on the Street, programmed trading I think. Fancies himself a merchant prince."

"Gossip has it that there's bad blood between you, that you should be King instead of him."

"You saw the Champion's Combat. Usually, the way it works is that a Champion fights for his liege lord. Philip screwed up. He thought I wasn't here. He had his new hard bod and three hundred and sixty-five days of training, so he stood for himself. When he fought me, he thought he would lose. Of course, he couldn't afford that, so he cheated."

"That stupid bastard!" Cass was surprised at the vehemence of his reply.

"Brian, he lusts to be High King. As a sworn knight in his demesne, I'm pledged to fight for him on Sunday in the Forest Battle, and help him win that crown!"

He shrugged sympathetically. "One of the harsher realities is that there are times when a person of honor is bound to one who has none."

" 'Mine honor is my life, both grow in one; take honor from me, and my life is done.' "

Brian chuckled. "I'll presume your brain intact if you can quote my old friend Will." He turned serious then and asked gently, "Now, Cassie, tell me about the horsemen."

"And out from the clouds of the storm-tossed sky—or would the roiling black of the abyssal pit be more appropriate?—came Mharyon and his Riders of the Shadows."

"You may mock, lass, but they spilled your blood."

"Look, Brian," she said wearily. "I've been coming to this War for years, it's always been fun, a way to live for a week in a world like that of the characters I write, and hang with my old college friends. Now all of a sudden, there're assholes running around looking to hurt people with their swords, riding the closest thing to a war charger this side of *Ivanhoe*, casting *spells* . . . I get the feeling I'm not in Kansas anymore, and I want to click my heels and go home.

"Then again, I could just be daft. Overworked, overtired, my imagination's running riot, my battered brain can't tell the difference anymore between fantasy and reality! I'm the only one who saw the Riders, maybe I am off my nut."

"Cass, if you talk long and loud and glibly enough, you can convince yourself of anything. But I twice saw the churned-up ground from a band of horsemen, and I see how cleanly the cut was made on your head."

She sighed and staggered over to the tiny camp table, waving for Brian to stay where he was, aiming for his bottle. She poured a finger of malt, hesitated, then added two more. As she picked up the tumbler she noticed her hand was trembling. She hoped it was fatigue, a residue from her impromptu swim, but knew most of it was fear. She hadn't realized how much she'd wanted to be believed, or how grateful she was that he did.

"Assuming you're right," she told Brian while clambering back onto the camp cot, "what's this all about?"

"I don't know, but I aim to learn."

"Okay, let's drive to the hospital and check up on that kid. Maybe—"

"No. That's not where the answers lie."

"Brian, I need to do something!"

"Then get your proper rest. I've a feeling you'll soon be needing it. In the meantime, I'll leave you with some words from an even older bard than yours: 'Among all men on the earth bards have a share of honor and reverence, because the muse has taught them songs and loves the race of bards.' "

"Whazzat?" Cass asked, stifling a yawn.

"Homer. It means get your rest, we may yet have need of you."

The sun was well up when Cass awoke, feeling rested. *Except for the aches, strains, cuts, and bruises,* Cass thought, *I feel like a million bucks!*

Brian was long gone and she helped herself to a pair of shorts to go with the T-shirt she'd slept in. Her knee still ached, but felt much better than she'd expected as she looked around the well-ordered tent for the remnants of her lovely costume. She found it all, a tangled mess of beads and cloth, carefully folded and laid in a box. *How like him,* she thought, *to take so much care.* And wondered how she could be so certain about someone she'd only just met.

Wishing for her shades to guard against the brilliant sun, she made her way to Annie's tent, to face her wrath. Gone was the joy of yesterday. Walking through the camp, looking at all the people dressed up and acting out, she just felt bone-tired.

And violated. Fieran's lying and cheating to win the crown Cass could at least understand. Aiming to have her disgraced she could understand. It was ego, the politics of power, and while Cass didn't like it, she knew where it came from.

This Mharyon, though, and his Riders. It had Fieran written all over it. She was certain it was Fieran down by the river. Damn him! The key to the War was that it was high adventure without threat of actual harm. Accidents, yes, but this was deliberate. For him to put that boy at risk—and worse, bring in a troop of thugs to guarantee his victory on Sunday—that was not only a violation of the Society's most fundamental rules, but of the trust pledged by every soul present. She couldn't think of a more basic betrayal of his coronation oath as King.

Cass pushed her way through the crowd around the barn. She bumped into people but took no notice, she was so engrossed in her thoughts. One look at her face and people gave her wide berth, this tall, angry woman with the bristling black hair.

Cass pushed through the door to Annie's tent, cast a murderous gaze at the couple looking at costumes. They beat feet fast, with mumbled apologies. Anne, knowing Cass better, just planted herself in her way, looked her in the eyes, and said, "What's wrong?"

Cass tossed the open box of ruined finery at her. Then collapsed on a pillow, the fight gone out of her, and said in the most sad of voices, "It didn't work, Annie."

Anne held up the bits of pieces of the costume, taking inventory of the tears, noting the stains, finally holding up the damaged coif. She looked at her friend and, fearing the worst, asked softly, "What happened?"

So Cass told her, in bits and pieces, helped along by sips of iced tea and the warmth of Anne's compassion. She told Anne of the nightmare of being chased through the woods and then being accosted by a group of men. The most frightening thing for her was that the situation had been totally out of her control; it was only by their will that she emerged more or less unharmed.

She looked up at her old friend. "Annie, I tried. I wore the costume and it was swell. I even had a great time walking through the Barn. But I can't get over the feeling—no, dammit, the certainty—that if I'd been dressed as a warrior, wearing my sword, that asshole would never have considered me easy pickings."

"So that's the answer? Always wear armor?" Anne asked mildly.

"Dammit, it wasn't funny! Maybe it was playacting for those guys, for me it was real. I could have gotten killed out there."

"Cass, don't you see? The answer is not for you to always be on the defensive. If you want to play, here, at least, you should be allowed to play. Scheherazade, Sleeping Beauty, Bugs Bunny if you like. Look, did you like the costume?"

"Yeah," Cass admitted sheepishly.

"Then I'll fix it, even if you only wear it in the comfort of your boudoir. You should have that right. And as for the rough trade in the forest, we'll take care of them."

Cass gave Anne a hug, and then spent the next several hours lolling on pillows, trying on clothes, drinking iced tea, and gossiping with her friend. If the Society had places for people like Annie, perhaps there was some hope for it.

⚜

It was deep purple twilight when Cass returned to her campsite. Preparations for dinner were already well under way and no one appeared interested in her offer to help, so she retired to her tent to change. As she rummaged in her case for fresh clothes, she caught sight of her sword lying on the bed. Though it was worn about the encampment only for show, she knew it had been forged as well as any true weapon. The balance was superb, the edge keen; it would give a good account of itself in any fight. She was tempted to carry it tonight, it would look like part of a costume, but then thought better of it. Whacking some poor idiot who plucked her too taut nerves was not something she wanted on her conscience.

She remembered the dream of Mharyon on the tor—hand unconsciously tightening on the haft and bringing the sword out of its scabbard and up to an *en garde* position—and rubbed the heel of her palm against her breast, aware of a dull ache deep within the bone, a resonance of her earlier nightmare. In her mind's eye she could see herself and Mharyon crossing swords, her lighter steel shattering under the impact of his black blade, her arm smashed aside by his far greater strength; she saw herself fall in a shower of blood, and opened her eyes wide to thrust away the fantasy image of her own death.

There were tears on her cheeks and her nose was stuffed. Cass snuffled loudly and wiped her nose clean.

The night had grown chill and Cass was cold—*from all my impromptu swim dates*, she told herself deliberately. Reaching into her duffel for the warmest clothes

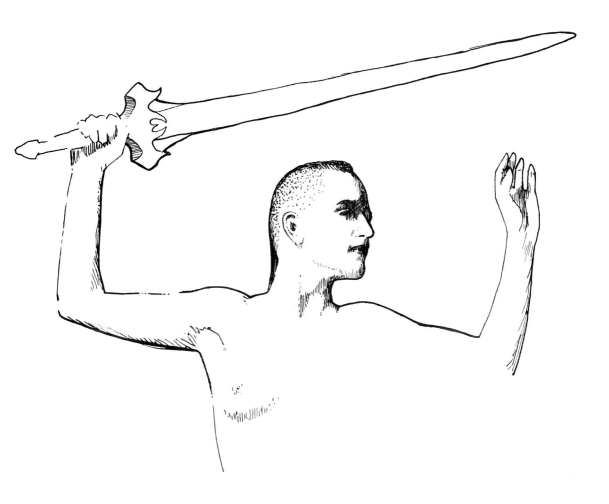

that came to hand without caring if they were period or not, she emerged in leather trousers and boots, a hand-knit Aran sweater, and her caracalla cloak. Dani had left a pack of cigarettes on the table and she bummed one.

"I thought you'd quit," Lynn chided, watching Cass rummage through the coolers piled off to one side.

"I did," Cass replied.

"Ah. This have anything to do with yesterday?"

Cass didn't know how to answer, didn't know where to begin. She sighed, sat on the cooler, and improvised, "Just boys, I guess, and life, and my old age."

"This wouldn't have anything to do with where you spent last night, would it? Although I doubt that Brian Griffin qualifies as a boy."

Cass looked at her incredulously. "God, Lynn, you gotta be joking." Her friend shook her head. Cass sighed. "Okay, you're not joking. Look, scout's honor, I don't have anything going with him."

"You better tell George. He's worried."

The need to explain herself on top of all her other concerns just made Cass mad. "Look, I'm thirty-five years old and having my midlife crisis. I don't have to answer to him. He's not my brother!"

Lynn looked at her sharply. "Cass, I'm pretty sure he knows that."

Cass refused to hear what Lynn was saying, and so changed the subject. "What's to drink?"

"Beer, soda, wine—the usual."

Cass noisily rummaged around in the cooler, hoping to put off more questions from Lynn. There was an open bottle of white, but Cass opted for some Coke instead. She yearned for the oblivion of being dead drunk, yet with all the uncertainties that faced her, she wanted to remain fully alert, in complete control of her faculties.

As she took her first hit off the can, making a face as some fizz went down the wrong way, she noticed George and Stefan off a little ways where there was more room, stretching a fitted percale bedsheet on a rude wooden frame, while Bosche used a can of spray paint to draw the crude silhouette of what Cass deduced was a man. It wasn't until he added a halo that things began to make sense. She wandered over for a closer look.

"Any of you stalwarts care to enlighten me . . . ?"

"*Hah!*" Bosche cried. "Already our Sacred Shroud works its blessed magic, our friend has risen from her sick—nay, her deathbed—and has returned to us!"

"Say *what!*"

George gave her a long look, and Cass hoped he hadn't overheard her conversation with Lynn. But after a moment he just grinned, and announced in his most rumbly *basso profundo* voice, "Behold, the Sacred Shroud of Padua." On cue, Lynn and Dani chimed in with an appropriate celestial fanfare. Cass hated them when they did that, they were always in tune; she herself sang about as well as a frog.

George took her by the hand and led her to the sheet. "Note, if you will, gentle lady, the fine workmanship, the delicate and subtle arrangement of the flowers imprinted on the cloth, their vibrant colors, how closely, one might say intimately, the very threads lie together. And indeed, how splendidly those of polyester mimic their forebears of base cotton."

He raised his voice for the benefit of the crowd gathering 'round. "This is no ordinary sheet, but is in fact the very one 'pon which the Sacred Shell of our Lord was lain, lo those many centuries agone, on a hitherto unsuspected visit to a Holiday Inn in Upper Galilee. He would've made a better impression," he continued *sotto voce*, "but he rolled over inna middle of the night and fell off. Still, who are we to quibble with a miracle?"

"Who, indeed?" Cass laughed. "You know this is very silly. What are you going to do with it?"

"Make the rounds of the camp tonight, bless the sick, hand out holy relics."

"Huh?"

Lynn picked an open, shallow box off the table; cardboard dividers separated it into compartments, in which, Cass was told with great solemnity, were the sacred bones of Saint Francis of Perdue ("last night's roast chicken dinner"), the remnants of Lot's wife, found near the legendary site of Sodom and Gomorrah ("rock salt from a hardware store in Hoboken"), wood shavings from the true cross ("not all the firewood went into the fire"), straw from the blessed manger, guaranteed slept on by real animals (Cass didn't need to be told where that came from, she'd walked through enough of it over the past two days), and apple cores from the Garden of Eden (indeed, Bosche finished the apple he was eating and added it to the collection, explaining deadpan that Eve must have been awfully hungry that fateful afternoon). Cass shook her head in wonderment; this was just what she needed, this was the War the way it should be.

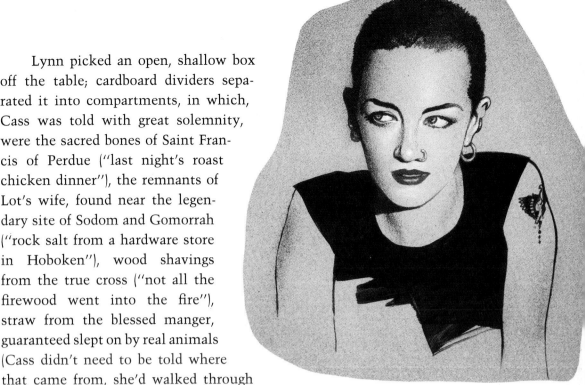

Everyone lined up on the road, Bosche carrying the Sacred Shroud, Lynn the box of holy relics. Stefan carried a lantern hung at the end of a pole while Dani danced alongside banging on her tambourine. Off they went, George and Cass in the lead, faking fanfares with their voices, Cass calling on all within hearing in her broadest Cockney to "Bring out'cher dead!" Every so often, they stopped and ran through their spiel, Cass improvising to fit the audience. Lynn "sold" relics, Dani danced away, Cass the raconteur spun out her nonsense, George, Bosche, and Stefan stalwartly held the Shroud. Fiercely happy, Cass thought, *These are my friends.*

People looked at them as if they were crazy, pushed past in a hurry, obviously with something much better to do; inspected relics, laughed, made offerings; joined the procession. They roamed the camp, cheerfully irreverent and disrespectful, shamelessly pitching to all they could find.

"Milords, ladies and gentlemen," Cass proclaimed to a likely-looking crowd, "I bid you all pay heed as we present unto you this most holy artifact, the Sacred Shroud of Padua. Say Amen, children!"

"Amen!" chimed George, Bosche, Stefan, Lynn, and Dani on cue.

"Brought forth from the land of Wamsutta, liberated from the dread hordes of Kmart, many are the miles and most cruel the adversities that have been endured by this most wondrous relic. But all that is past, and now the Shroud has been brought forth among this gathering, now, for a limited time only, direct to you!"

Children giggled, grown-ups laughed, a few even came forward to haggle good-humoredly over the rising cost of relics. Standing next to George, his arm thrown around her, Cass smiled.

"Become a palmist, Milady Siobhan? My, how the mighty have fallen."

Cass whirled around to find Fieran in all his kingly finery, smugly ensconced among his entourage, a smile on his lips.

"You know the old saying, Fieran—Better to serve heaven than rule hell," Cass replied, a nasty grin on her face. "I thought to pledge holy orders, have my sword serve God instead of your demesne."

"Tut, tut, milady, we couldn't permit that. Honor has pledged your sword to me." His lips still smiled, but his eyes grew rock hard. In the eyes of the gathering assemblage, he had a lot to lose if the Lady Siobhan withdrew her support. He knew it, she knew it.

"Ah, Philip, you speak to me of honor?" she asked in a deceptively light tone, deliberately using his workaday name.

"Show some respect, milady. The proper form of address is 'Your Majesty'!" one of his entourage shouted hotly.

"Y'know, Philip, it's guys like him"—she jerked her thumb at his attendant—"working for guys like you that give revolution a good name. Sorry, fellas, we're fresh out of respect tonight. Just consider us your basic narco-syndicalist collective."

"Bloody peasant!" Fieran, not totally dim, got the reference.

George stepped up, hoping to defuse the situation. "Excuse me, are we about to see some repression of the masses?" he asked, turning on a deliberately thick comic-Brit accent.

"Perhaps later, Faraday," Fieran answered, honing the edge to his voice. "Only if you behave. Perhaps we'll play Spanish Inquisition. A nice *auto-da-fé* might make a surprisingly pleasant diversion.

"In the meantime, though, We would like to offer an appropriately Royal tithe. For victory in battle." He locked eyes with Cass while handing over a wad of paper to George.

"Drink tickets for the Barn. The peasants rejoice."

Fieran raised his voice for the crowd, once more falling into the role of benef-icent monarch. "Eat, drink, and make merry, gentles all—"

"—For tomorrow we shall surely die." George cheerily finished the quote, then noticed Cass had gone white and was edging out of the torchlight, away from her friends. He caught up to her, but she chose not to hear him calling, not until he touched her shoulder. "You okay?"

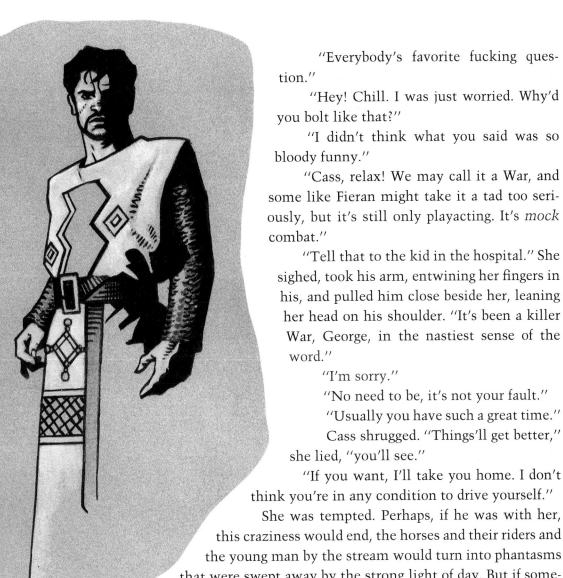

"Everybody's favorite fucking question."

"Hey! Chill. I was just worried. Why'd you bolt like that?"

"I didn't think what you said was so bloody funny."

"Cass, relax! We may call it a War, and some like Fieran might take it a tad too seriously, but it's still only playacting. It's *mock* combat."

"Tell that to the kid in the hospital." She sighed, took his arm, entwining her fingers in his, and pulled him close beside her, leaning her head on his shoulder. "It's been a killer War, George, in the nastiest sense of the word."

"I'm sorry."

"No need to be, it's not your fault."

"Usually you have such a great time."

Cass shrugged. "Things'll get better," she lied, "you'll see."

"If you want, I'll take you home. I don't think you're in any condition to drive yourself."

She was tempted. Perhaps, if he was with her, this craziness would end, the horses and their riders and the young man by the stream would turn into phantasms that were swept away by the strong light of day. But if something were about to happen, how would George feel knowing that she had run away? All her stories revolved around the fundamental values of friendship and honor; if they were a true reflection of her self, of Cass Dunreith's soul, how could she leave? Or were those professed beliefs as much a fantasy as the stories?

Without warning, she found herself falling, her arms tightening about George's torso as her leg hooked his out from under him, the two of them tumbling off the road and down the shallow slope of the field behind the last line of tents. As they hit, her conscious mind registered what her subconscious had reacted to: the braying laughter of a Rider, pinned by the stab of his eyes, the flash of his ax blade in the firelight as he raised it high overhead, slashing toward Cass and George. He missed—barely—deliberately. A wind followed in his wake, snapping pennants and

torch flames, blowing some out and filling the air with dust. She saw him ride howling *through* a crowd of people without any of them noticing, raucous laughter hissed on the wind, and then he disappeared into the night. *A ghost,* she thought sickly, *a fantasy, without the power to harm anyone, only to scare me. Worked, too, the fucker.*

"Cass!" George squawked.

She levered herself off him and sprawled on her back on the grass, staring up at the stars, wondering how she was going to explain her actions.

"You're crying," he said in amazement, confusion and concern replacing anger.

"It's been that kind of night, Rags. Did I hurt you?"

"Hardly. Just knocked a little wind out of me. Nice move."

"I thought I . . . saw something."

"What?"

"A six-foot-tall guy in armor, on a horse, swinging a battle-ax for your head."

"Shit."

"You believe me?"

"I wish I could. But if you ask me, you got out of bed *way* too soon. I don't care what that guy Brian says, you should be in a hospital. Who the hell is he anyway, where does he get off taking such a proprietary interest in your life?"

"At the time, he seemed like a lifesaver."

"Well, I don't trust him. He appears out of nowhere, no one knows who he is." He stopped abruptly, but obviously wanted to say more. He got to his feet and held out his hand.

"What's that for?"

"I'll walk you back to your tent."

"And tuck me in for the night?"

"Whatever. I'm at your disposal."

She hugged him—that kind of blind generosity was just what she needed. "That's sweet, Rags. It means a lot to me. But I'm too wired to sleep, I can't sit, I need to move. I think I'll head up to the Barn and dance. Achy-breaky knee and all." She offered a smile.

"Want company?"

"Not quite yet. Go join the others, they're probably wondering where we've got to, and one of us has to burst their fantasies."

"That seems a shame."

"Trust me, sport," she said lightly. "It's more for your reputation than mine. I'll be along, really. Just now, though, I need some time to think."

George shoved some of the scrip given to him by Fieran into her hand. "Take this, then. If you want to do yourself damage, at least you won't have to pay for it."

Cass stood looking after him, watched him stride purposefully away. She hoped she hadn't hurt his feelings too badly, taken too much advantage of an old friend. Then she took a long, slow turn—her eyes set, her expression grim—sweeping over the camp as though scouting for the slightest sign of an enemy.

⚜

The set ended, and the band left the stage for a much-needed break. Cass thanked her latest dance partner and returned—albeit unsteadily, from an equally delicious mix of exhaustion and drink—to her table. The exertion had done her more good than she had thought possible, and she positively beamed when she caught sight of the back of a tall, well-built man in black silk and leather—the cut of his clothes very much a match of her own—seated in the chair opposite hers.

Until he turned at the sound of her approach and she saw who it was.

Mharyon drained the last of the beer in her mug and set it on the table.

"An adequate brew," he said, making his dismissal plain.

She forced herself to stand and face him, when every instinct screamed, *Run!* She couldn't tell what was on her face, but her heart was beating like a runaway trip-hammer; there was too much tension in her hands for the fingers to even shake.

"I suppose you can do better," she replied, and marveled at how casual she sounded.

"For beer, what's the point?" He rose and indicated the seat opposite.

Cass couldn't walk away. She was drunk and cocky, her curiosity too great.

"I can, however, offer wine as an alternative." Cass cocked an eyebrow as his sudden sleight of hand deposited two tumblers on the table. He lifted a tooled-leather wineskin with silver mounts from the floor and filled both. Despite herself, Cass was impressed by the workmanship of the wineskin; the artisans here numbered among the best in the country, yet she knew none of them could craft a piece like this, though some would break their heart—or, the wayward and disturbing thought struck her, *sell their soul*—to try.

"Forgive my presumption," Mharyon said as he handed her a mug, "but since you accept my wine, I trust you'll do the same for my company."

Warning bells rang in her head. Cass warily but politely declined, and made do with more beer from her pitcher. "It's not safe to mix one's drinks. Or, some say, to talk with strangers." She looked at him over the top of her mug.

That didn't appear to bother him in the slightest as he slouched in his chair with his long powerful legs outstretched and surveyed the crowded hall. "Milady, you forget, out of all others here, you and I are not strangers. Cousins, perhaps, but never strangers." And he tossed her a winning smile.

Against her better judgment, her anger welled up at this man's cavalier manners. "My family doesn't take to chasing each other through the woods with swords."

He smiled wolfishly in genuine amusement. "You doubt me still, Cass Dunreith?"

"At this point, pal, I find myself doubting everything."

"I had a run-in with one of your boys a little while ago." She took another swallow at the memory. "It was Finn, I think, the yob who tried to claim me down by the creek." Mharyon's mouth twisted in disapproval. "I felt the hiss of his ax as it missed me. I heard his laugh. I even smelled his damn horse!

"But no one else did. Not even the man right beside me. Your Rider was as real as this table, but I saw him gallop straight through a mob of people, actually *through* them!"

He said nothing, allowing her the next move.

"I hope I'm losing my mind, sport. I don't much care for the alternative."

"Which is?" he wondered aloud, daring her to answer.

"I should call the cops. At the very least, the Council of Kings. You have no right to be here!"

"Quite the contrary, I—and mine—have more right than most. You were there; we were summoned."

"This is idiotic." Cass leaned forward, the alcohol burned from her blood. "You look like an intelligent man. Take your people and go. This life that you're living is for us just a game. Everyone here will think you deranged."

"You do yourself no good service with such talk, Lady."

There was a burst of noise from the dance floor, a sudden squeal of laughter as a woman was swept into the air by a burly barbarian and then handed off to an even bigger companion. The woman's dance partner made a move to protest and Cass half rose from her chair as the mood twisted toward something ugly. Words were exchanged, along with a couple of shoves. The woman now looked scared. The barbarians were wearing steel, daggers of various sizes and antecedents, and as Cass watched in mounting concern, wondering where she could find a weapon of her own, hands moved oh-so-casually to cover hilts. Then the lead barbarian shoved a tankard of ale into the man's grasp. As quickly as that, the mood changed again, the tension evaporating from the scene, the challenges resolved by good-natured back-pounding and bellybumping.

Trembling, Cass looked around the Barn, and saw that only she had reacted as if anything was the slightest bit amiss.

Her gaze returned to Mharyon, who was still in his seat. "Make things better, then," she told him flatly.

"It can't be helped. The spirit rubs off us like hair from a cat."

"You said we were kin," Cass said.

"That is why you alone have safe conduct from this place."

She stared at him, until he dropped his eyes and finished his drink.

"The boy told Fieran he had a means to guarantee him, not only the throne of a Domain, but the High Crown as well. Is that it, is that why you're here?"

"The musicians have returned, milady." Mharyon rose to his feet, giving the impression that he was towering over her. He held out a hand. "Will you join me?"

As before, with the offer of wine, the force of his personality was such that her body responded of its own volition, her own hand halfway to his, a willing—almost eager—assent on her lips, before she caught herself. She felt a flush of heat deep within herself, a resonance of her dream, as though her insides had been recast in molten flesh.

"For the dance alone," she answered carefully. "And in return for my favor, I ask you one. That you answer my questions."

Mharyon's smile was relaxed and confident, yet Cass wondered why alarms were sounding from her head to her toes. Was she misreading him, was the danger imaginary, was his just another persona, but with a strange sense of play?

"Fair enough," he said.

The music was Celtic rock, the songs a mix of classic folk and more modern tunes. The one constant was that they created an irresistibly infectious impulse to dance. As Cass could have guessed, Mharyon was poetry in motion. His movements were primal and passionate, athletic to excess, and Cass with her bad knee found herself hard-pressed to keep up. His night-dark hair framed his achingly handsome face, his leather-clad hips pitched and swayed, and his gray eyes were for her alone. Through some trick of voice, despite the terrific din, his every word came to Cass as though the room were dead silent, all the others present just props for the scene about to be played.

"In the oldest days," he said, pulling her so tight against his silk-covered chest that Cass could smell his scent of ferns and fresh heather, before she spun herself away to the full length of their arms, "the Shadow Riders and their lord were warriors of Faery. They rode the Wild Hunt and stood beside the Highest of the High. Some tales have them descended from the dark Germanic gods, Wodan and his Pack, but in truth they are far older."

His scent was intoxicating, the muscles rippling through his body mesmerizing; she was entering a realm of the senses alone. "Few, eldritch or human, could match their fury in battle; as a consequence, the Riders were treated with the utmost respect. Only Royalty could summon them, and then only in the time of greatest peril, for the honor of their service merited only the most precious of gifts in return.

"The Riders are bound by a code of conduct that is older than your history. In that lies both the greatest safety and the greatest danger.

"They are proud, my Riders, beyond your powers of description or comprehension. They are not summoned casually. Only a fool would treat them with disrespect."

The melody of his voice lulled her, the warmth of his body soothed her, but now the content of his words hit home. She pushed away from him. "You have it all so neatly tied, by rules no one knows but you. Do those who summon you know that this bargain was struck?"

"Tell me, Cass, does the blame in this fall to those who remain true to their beliefs, or those who've profaned them?"

He pulled her close again, their bodies melding with a fluid intensity that left her gasping. She stepped away, he followed, their movements twinned, as though the dance had been choreographed for them. As the music built to its crescendo, so did they, no more words spoken between them for a time, all their talk done with hands and eager bodies.

"We are well met, you and I," he said softly when the set ended, no touch needed, only a look, to send a frisson of raw electricity surging between them.

"I . . . " she began, and then took a deep, shuddering breath. "I don't think so."

She wound her way back to their table and poured another mug of beer from her pitcher. She didn't drink any of it, though, but straightened to her full height—deliberately matching her presence to his—as she sensed his silent approach behind her.

"Gifts, you said?" she demanded. "That's what it'll take to buy you off?"

"Not in the way you mean."

He stepped around into her field of view and continued speaking. "Consider them a gesture of respect, from one power to another. An acknowledgment of forces that reach beyond this waking world."

"I don't understand."

"The gifts could be symbolic or real. It was never the offering itself, per se, but rather the spirit in which it was made."

"The blood of Kings, to fructify the earth."

"A sacrifice, yes."

"A blood offering, you mean? A *life*? Mharyon, I was talking about practices common over a thousand years ago."

"The times may change, Cass, not the rules we live by."

Her arm moved of its own volition, snapping forward to hurl the contents of her mug full into this lunatic's face. But then she brought the mug back, to stare at it in thunderstruck disbelief; what had been a simple ceramic vessel had become a hollow skull, the bone polished so smooth that it gleamed like ivory, its features decorated with an elegant filigree of entwined gold and silver, the eye sockets gleaming with mother of pearl.

She looked at Mharyon, and saw his was no different; the two skulls might have been a matched pair.

"A noble foe," he said simply. "May that I find such here."

68

She flung the cup aside, heard it explode against the wall with force enough to turn heads her way and provoke a flurry of comments. No one had seen the reason for her action, only the act itself.

She didn't care. Now, at last—*and way too late,* she thought—she made her break for the door, radiating such red rage that everyone in her path scrambled to give her the widest possible berth.

She burst into the open air, chest heaving, casting about wildly for a path through the crowd outside. She was aching to hit somebody, and when Mharyon caught hold of her arm, she tried to do precisely that, with a sloppy, roundhouse swing that he evaded easily, slapping the punch aside and gathering her close against him in a way that tangled both arms and legs and left her pinned. She didn't like that. He ignored her protests.

"You asked of the Riders, Cass. I am telling you. Would you rather I lie?"

"Damn you, Mharyon, let me go!"

"As you wish, milady."

He released her and she staggered forward a brace of awkward steps. She should have fallen, but managed to recover herself and confront him.

"I have news for you, O Highborn Lord," she snarled, her voice harsh in her own ears. "Fieran is no true King. He's just a little man with a big ego who lied to win the Champion's Combat. And by summoning you, by violating the Society's covenant, he foreswore any claim he had to *either* crown! He may think he's king of the hill, but it's a hill of bullshit." She spat on the ground and glared Mharyon in the eye. "By your own rules, you're doubly betrayed! What say that to your ancient honor?"

His eyes were angry, dead mad, but his voice was cool and even detached. "If so, a proper price would be demanded. And paid. This War of yours, cousin"—and he waved his arms wide to encompass the whole encampment—"suppose it were no longer pretend?"

"What, you have the power to make it real?" Cass scoffed. But when their eyes met this time, the derision died in her throat; without altering form or feature in the slightest, Mharyon had *changed.* Suddenly he looked unhuman, of a race and age she'd known only in her dreams.

When he spoke, it was as sovereign passing sentence, in a hollow ringing voice: "When the trumpet sounds the start of the Forest Battle, and the first blow is struck, rattan will become steel. Blunt weapons will grow the sharpest of edges. Warriors will bleed and die. They will not be able to stop themselves. And those who triumph will celebrate that victory by sweeping through this camp like the hordes of ancient days. The blood fever, the lust, will touch all present; none will escape and only one survive."

"Why," Cass cried, "because I'm bloody *kin*?"

"Let's just call it your birthright, cousin."

"I'll have the camp closed down, you son of a bitch, and everyone sent home!"

"For what cause? Out of fear of a band of wild horsemen that only you have ever seen? And even if you're believed—even if these Riders are all you say they are—they're but a score against thousands. Surely, among this entire multitude, there should be warriors and true weapons sufficient to stop them. Surely some will be eager to try."

"I'll find a way, damn you!"

"Here, Cassandra, your name betrays you. Look around. Cry all the warnings you wish, until heart and voice together crack, none will believe, because this is what they want. Nothing will be offered that is not, in some measure—great or small—already desired."

"Bastard," she whispered, pale as death and swaying as though from a physical blow, because casting across her mind was a taunting refrain, *He's right, you know, you've walked this road before,* that found full voice in a primal shriek, "You motherless *bastard*!"

"In blood were the Riders summoned. In blood must we be appeased. Consider us the proudest of a proud folk, milady; we have never taken our role lightly. And have less reason in this age that denies our very being to forgive even a slight transgression."

With a battle cry that sent many within earshot grabbing reflexively for their weapons, Cass launched herself at him—only to be thrown roughly to the ground and pinned facedown in the dirt, held in a hammerlock that was meant to hurt.

"All may well be as you've said, Cass Dunreith," he told her, his impassive expression belied by a sad undertone, "and what you so desperately wish to believe. Perhaps I am simply mad, or a hallucination, or the product of your own madness."

"No!"

"Or it could be truth."

He released her and stepped quickly back out of reach. She didn't move, choosing to lie where she fell, hugging the ground as though both life and soul depended on it, sobbing silent tears of rage and pain, and a grief mingled with no little shame, emotions born of memories and guilt buried so deep she had no true idea of them. There was smoke in her eyes, too much for the torches and fires burning nearby, and a mingled taste and stench so foul she didn't want to know more. She kept her eyes tight shut, wishing for some way to block the sound of him as well, as her imagination turned his sketch of words into a full-blown painting.

"You have no place here, child of an ancient name," he said. "You cannot share their fate."

He knelt by her side and began a gesture that was meant to comfort, only to think better of it, choosing to caress with voice instead of hand.

"Leave, Cassandra," he said, with a lover's tenderness, "while you're still able."

She pushed herself up to her knees, casting about for him, but he was gone. She searched for him, first with a turn of the head, then ever more frantically calling his name over and over.

"For god's sake, *Cass*!"

She blinked, blinked again in confusion as her gaze went to the face of her friend Anne. She knelt with Cass on the ground, held her by both shoulders, with a strength well hidden by her plump frame.

"My god," Cass breathed, staring about herself in disbelief, to find the world as it was supposed to be.

"Is everything okay? Are you all right? Who was that guy!"

"Dear me, milady Siobhan, feeling a touch unstable this evening? Perhaps I should not have been so generous with my largess?"

She looked blearily up at Fieran, looming over her with entourage in tow.

"Perhaps I should have left you some of your Sacred Shroud's sacred relics, you certainly look like you need something."

She didn't bother rising, knelt in the dirt wild-eyed, but gathered about her an aspect of self that prompted the King to wrap his cloak tight about his own body. "Poor Philip," she said, in an eerie, keening voice that came from some ancient lost place in her Highland soul. "Your reign is pitiful, your heart untrue, your kingdom lost through your liar's tongue. Wrap the tatters of your kingship hard about you, for soon it will be but a revenant tossed on the wind."

"You threatening me, Dunreith?" His voice cracked as he addressed the growing crowd. "You all heard, you're all witnesses!" He rounded dramatically on Cass, but took a startled step backward as he found her on her feet. "Keep talking, sweetheart, keep acting this way, you'll find yourself banned! Not only from this War, but from the Society itself! I mean it. I can do it!"

But he was yelling that last to her back. Without a look to him, Cass turned and walked away.

⚜

She slung a satchel over her shoulder as she emerged from her tent—she'd looked long and hard at her blades, debating whether to bring them as well, then decided against it—and, to her joy, crashed full tilt into George.

"Rags!"

"Damn you, Cass!" he raged at her, mixing confusion with outright anger. "What the hell's gotten into you tonight? You got any idea of the stories I've heard?"

"Probably no worse than the ones I've told over the years."

"This isn't funny, Cass!"

"No shit, Sherlock."

He took her by the shoulders to give her a hearty shake, but she broke his grip, so that the two of them stood toe to toe, glaring at each other.

"Goddammit, will you *listen* to me," he said, as shaken as she was by how quickly this little confrontation had flared almost out of control.

"Fieran's claiming you're having some kind of breakdown," he rushed on. "He isn't coming right out and saying it, but he's leaving the clear impression that you're responsible for whatever happened to that kid you found down by the river. He wants the docs to call the paramedics to take *you* to the hospital."

"Loony bin, no doubt."

"I'm serious, woman—and so is he! And I gotta tell ya, Cass, the way you're acting, he may have a point! I've never seen you like this, you're scaring people."

"I'm scared myself, Rags." She held out her keys. "Look, you said you'd drive me home, that offer still good?"

"You want to pack your stuff?"

"I have what I need." She patted the satchel. "Look, I just want to *go,* is that all right? Please, George, let's get in my car and roll."

"Okay, okay, I'm coming! Lemme just leave a note for the others."

"Any hope of getting them to come with, maybe?"

He looked up from his scribbling.

"You got me, kiddo, don't push your luck."

The words came back to haunt them both when the Volkswagen reached the bridge. It spanned the stream that handled the lake's outflow and was normally the most placid and well behaved of watercourses. Now they stood before a raging torrent that was level with the bridge itself and overflowing its banks for some fair distance, with such force that neither felt inclined to try a crossing in a vehicle, much less on foot. They could hear the timbers groan with strain; the bridge was stoutly constructed but it was doubtful it could long withstand such pressure.

"I don't believe this!" George exclaimed. "There's been rain, but I'd say nothing like what's needed to produce a flood like this. In all the years I've been coming to the War, I've never seen the water so high, or so rough."

"Lake's higher than ever," Cass commented. "Heard that from the caretaker, it's been that way all spring. And you've seen the cataracts. Still, it was fine here yesterday."

"It ain't fine anymore, Cass. I guess we're stuck for the duration."

"The hell we are!" She rounded on him in determination. "The interstate's a quarter mile through those woods. There's an emergency phone near the camp turn-off; we can call for help!"

"Call who? What for?"

"Humor me, okay? C'mon!"

She struck off across the parking field without a backward glance, certain he'd follow, daring him not to. In fact, he stood his ground for the better part of a minute, torn with indecision, until friendship got the better of him. With a grumble of self-disgust he backed the car into a parking space and took off after her at a lumbering jog.

"If I didn't know better," he huffed as he caught up to her, "I'd be thinking right now that Fieran maybe has a point."

She shot him a jaundiced, sideways glance, but didn't break her stride, daring him to keep pace.

"That why you're tagging along, then," she shot back, "to protect the loony from herself?"

"Cut me some slack, willya?"

"Likewise."

And with that, they were in among the trees. The ground cover was thick and tangled, there was no trail to be easily seen, and in a matter of steps they came almost to a dead stop. Trees towered above them on every side, obscuring any sight of sky overhead, the space between the trunks filled with branches grown so intertwined it was like trying to pick a path through a hedgerow. There was no way to mark a straight course; they'd hardly made any progress before they found themselves completely disoriented, without a clue as to the right direction to go. Cass tried her flashlight, but all the beam did was show the obstacles before them in greater detail.

"I think I like the woods better by daylight," George groused, not bothering to hide his unhappiness. He hated being hemmed in.

"Lions and tigers and bears, oh my . . . "

"Be just our luck to find all three," he said, refusing to be cheered.

"I can't even hear the interstate. We're not that far, there should be sounds of traffic."

"You hadn't heard? This year we've banned all modern influences for the duration, inside the camp and out." George was so locked into his own head, he missed the shocked, assessing look Cass gave him. "Fortunately," he pressed on, "those of us who were formerly of the Boy Scout persuasion have come, as always, prepared." With a smile that was merely an exercise in muscle management, he held up a compass.

But when they took a closer look, for a direction, even that faded.

"It's spinning," George said, pursing his lips. "The needle won't settle down, I can't get a decent bearing. Must be some iron ore deposits—stands to reason, this is old mining country."

"So why haven't we ever noticed the problem before?"

He glared at her, mostly in outrage, as though he thought that she thought that he was doing this on purpose. Or worse, that it was somehow her fault. They faced each other, neither speaking, until Cass realized that George had no intention of moving of his own volition. Here he stood, here he would stay. She would have to take the lead.

So she did, and he followed.

"Wish I could see some stars," he mused as they made their way through the underbrush. He wasn't talking to her, or even to himself; it was more on the order of whistling in a graveyard.

"Damn funny how thick this wood is. I've done my share of wanderings during other Wars, I don't recall it ever looking like this. And look at these trees—I mean, this is serious old-growth forest."

"Whole lotta chopsticks, all right."

A sudden, violent wind stirred the air and slapped at the pair of them, as though some great creature hadn't liked what it heard and had given them a sharp breath of warning.

"I dunno, Cass," said George carefully, "maybe that isn't such a popular sentiment in these parts. I sort of pity the poor guy who tries to lay an ax to a dryad's grove."

Another stir amid the trees, no comparison to the first, and Cass searched the shadows for the source of the tinkly, ghostly laughter.

"How long you figure we've been hiking? Man, from the way my feet and legs ache, must've been hours." With every sentence, he sounded more upset, and there was a whine to his voice Cass had never heard before. "You'd think we'd have reached the damn road by now."

"You'd think," she agreed, and then pointed. "Rags, the trees are thinning!"

He almost ran her down in his eagerness to take the lead. The going was markedly easier, the lay of the land and spacing between the trees much as Cass remembered them, as they burst into the open only to find themselves once more on the parking field.

"We must've gotten turned around somehow," George said.

Cass wasn't listening as she turned once more to the forest arrayed against her.

"Hey!" he called, clutching her by the arm. "Where are you going?"

"Where does it look like?"

"This is getting silly!" And his grip tightened enough to hurt. "Look, Cass, I don't know what you're afraid of, but it can't be that bad. Maybe now you've hiked some of that *agita* out of your system, you can come back to the camp, settle down by the fire. We can work through this."

"A little wine," she suggested, "perhaps some smoke, they'll drive the bogey-men away?" She pushed past the tree line, entered the woods.

"Something like that, yeah!" He sounded defensive. "You're not having fuck-all luck trying anything else tonight. For Christ's sake, Cass, look at yourself, *listen* to yourself! You know as well as I do, you're not acting rationally!"

"I guess it all depends on how you define the term." She twisted in his grasp, baring teeth as she broke herself free. He looked surprised—not so much at her escape but that he'd been holding her so hard. She watched him flex his hand, slowly closing it into a fist, as though to convince himself it was still his to command. "I'm done, Rags, I'm gone. I need you to come with me."

"I don't see why." And the deliberate bitterness was like a physical blow. "You haven't needed me all week. Fuck, I don't think you've needed anyone in your whole life!"

"Come with me, please," she was pleading. "I'll do anything, just come away from here."

"No. Not now." George put himself in her path, forcing her to a stop. "This place is magic, Cass, was magic for us. I can still feel it. I plan to stay."

"Dammit, Colin, don't *do* this to me! It's not magic, never was magic. Just death and despair and loneliness! Listen to me, *trust me*! Please! There's too much at stake!"

"Who the hell is Colin?"

"What did you say?"

"Colin. You called me Colin. Who's that, Cass? Another boyfriend who broke your heart? Another body to blame as you retreat deeper within yourself?"

It was as though he'd hit her, and the reply boiled up from some cold, cruel place deep within her, a rage stored up for most of her lifetime needing only this one small cut to set it loose.

"Fuck you," she said in a voice gone flat and toneless because there was no way it could express such pain and fury. She didn't know what he said in response, didn't hear, didn't care, as she broke for the trees at a run.

She went through the forest like a deer, a flat-out sprint without George to hold her back; some instinct showed her feet where to step, and her face to duck, to avoid the obstacles in her path, and in hardly any time at all she found herself on the broad, grassy verge that bordered the interstate. The road was still and empty, one of those rare moments when the tarmac clears to the horizon. Neither car nor truck in sight, and not even a hint of lights in the distance.

She didn't stop until she reached the phone and then it was as though she'd been tripped. Her feet went out from under her and she found herself stretched full length in the air for the split second it took her to crash to the ground. And once there, she didn't try to get up, but simply lay, hammering the earth again and again with a fist while she pulled the rest of her body into a tight little ball.

"No, George," she said, her voice breaking into sobs, "not a boyfriend. He was my brother."

⚜

She doesn't recognize the boy at first and decides to assume from the context that this is her brother. Almost three decades separate what she sees from the memory, and she can't help marveling at this vision of the other side of herself. Height isn't even there in promise, although the boy's bundled into an awkward, gangly precursor of her current rangy frame. It's hard to tell hair color from the light cast by the bare incandescent bulbs set at intervals along the stairway ceiling, wires anchored to the seam where stone wall and ceiling meet. There's reckless intelligence to his face, a fierce curiosity that promises trouble. He's just come from bed, very properly clad in pajamas and a tartan wool robe, wearing socks underneath his slippers against the nighttime chill. She should be dressed the same, but even then she never did. She looks the rowdy, but it's invariably Colin who plays the part.

She has the sense that he's hunting, and he reminds her of nothing so much as a young cat, exploring the boundaries of its world, in full certainty of its innate invulnerability. For some reason, she herself was never so confident. All about them is stone, an interior stairway curving up from shadows below to shadows beyond. A Victorian stair runner is an incongruous failure to add even a veneer of comfort to the space.

His grin of delight at seeing her makes her heart ache, striking resonances of memory that time and neglect have almost buried with dust. She reaches out to him, but he springs back and dashes up the stairs.

She calls after, then runs as the words trigger a sense of apprehension too urgent to be ignored. "Colin, don't! Remember what Daddy said!" That they were to stay in their rooms these nights—the words so clear, the look on his face so stern, like one of the ancestor portraits in the Great Hall, it's as though he's only just spoken. He wouldn't say why, only that it was important. Cass took him at his word. Colin, of course, saw it as a challenge.

"Come on, Cassie, you great, lumbering slowcoach!" his clear voice calls from above. "There's magic in the air, can't you feel it? Where's the harm in watching?"

"We're supposed to be in our room! Colin, this isn't right, you have to mind me, I'm the eldest!"

"By all of fifteen minutes!"

She's taking the steps two and three at a time, pushing hard enough to give her the beginnings of a muscle stitch along one side. She knows the castle layout, and nowhere is a stairwell this long; yet there's no end in sight, and no sign of Colin save his voice. And that, impossibly, is fading, as though he's pulling away. She redoubles her efforts, touched by an unaccountable dread. There's something in the air, but if it's magic she wants no part of it; the closest image that applies is music— rude, antagonistic, atonal chords that prick at her nerves like gnats. She and Colin are twins. How, she wonders—echoing in the adult a thought first had by the child—can a melody be so wonderful to one set of ears, so awful to another?

"Colin," she calls, "please! We were told to stay inside!"

"Cass, listen to the music!"

"I don't want to! It hurts! I don't like it, Colin, you mustn't listen, either!"

"If you don't like it, it's because you don't want to. Stop trying to spoil my fun!

"Oh, Cass, it's so beautiful!" From the wonder in his voice, she knows it is, and near chokes with bitterness at the unfairness of it all, that he can hear the glory and she can't.

"All I want to do is go out on the battlements, just for a little, to hear it better, just to see who's playing. It's so incredible, Cass, you've no idea! If you're scared, you go back to bed. I'll be all right."

"Colin," she calls, and then, in a full-throated scream, "Please, Colin!"

First she hears his merry, taunting, triumphant laughter. And feels the salt sting of hot tears on her cheeks. And then, with a suddenness that lashes at her like a horsewhip:

"Cassandra!"

She whirls about with such force that she loses her balance and thumps to her seat on the cold stone, cringing into the wall seam as children do when their parents announce themselves in the fullness of their wrath.

They're a handsome couple pounding up the stairs toward her, faces now familiar only from the precious photos in her scrapbook, of wedding and family trips;

Janet and Thomas Dunreith, younger then than Cass is now, in the hearty prime of life, the Highland laird and his lady.

Her voice is small, pitched higher than she can ever remember hearing. "I tried to stop him, Daddy. I tried my hardest, I even begged. Colin didn't care. He says there's music, he went out onto the battlements to hear it better."

Her father spares a look up the stairs, and now at last Cass understands the expression when his face turns past her toward his wife.

"Put Cass to bed," her father tells Janet, "and see she stays."

But Mother has other ideas. "So you can go out there alone?"

"There's no danger, Janet. Trust me."

"Daddy, no!" Cass cries, knowing a lie when she hears one. "Don't go out there, it's not safe!"

He kneels before her, fatherly words and comforting gestures. "Would you rather I leave your brother all alone, accushla, with none to stand beside him?"

Then he straightens to his full height, which is where Cass gets hers, the dark black-red hair coming from her mother.

"Wife," he says with curious formality, "do as I ask. Take your daughter away while I go for my son." Three steps take him out of sight around the curve of the stairwell, the sound of his passage fading almost as quickly.

Cass lunges after him, only to be caught by her mother. She struggles fiercely, with all her might, shrieking her rage and fear—and a grief bottled up for all the years since this awful night—calling out Colin's name, calling for her father, while her mother simply holds on, overmatching Cass's strength with her own until the storm passes. A fury this intense doesn't last long; the child simply hasn't the resources to sustain it, and an adult hasn't the focus. Cries turn to sobs, and sobs to simple tears, and then the two women just hold each other, Cass resting her head on her mother's shoulder.

"Cassie," Janet calls. But when she hears no response, "Cassandra!" She doesn't raise her voice, merely adds a bit of an edge to get her daughter's attention.

"Downstairs, my girl, at once! I'll be along directly, to tuck you snug abed."

"Mummy," Cass protests, "Daddy said!"

"I know," Janet says. She draws Cass to her feet, moving down a step so she can meet her daughter's face with a level gaze. "When I married your father, Cassandra," she goes on, "I swore to love him, and honor and cherish and obey. But to be true to the first, I must cast aside the last, no matter what the cost. Colin is our son, as you are our daughter—but Thomas is mine! I won't leave him alone, with none to stand beside him. Especially tonight."

"What is there about tonight?" A question never asked by the child; in the face of her mother's implacable will, Cass had simply done as she was told. "Mom, what's happening? Where are you going? What's out there?"

79

Janet smiles a sad farewell and embraces her daughter a final time. "Do as you're told, sweet. Come the sunrise, this will be nothing but a bad dream."

⚜

By sunrise, she was in the Factor's car, a Land Rover much like Brian's, bashed and battered as much by hard use as age, careering over winding Highland tracks more suited to sheep, at speeds more appropriate to a Formula One racecourse. She'd been bundled out of bed and into traveling clothes, with no answers for her questions and an air of grim intensity that silenced even the thought of protest.

By midmorning, she'd crossed the border into England. And before another nightfall was on a BOAC Bristol *Britannia* flight out of Heathrow for New York. She'd never been back, to Britain or her Highland home.

⚜

She went into his tent like a ghost, with only a flashing wedge of moonlight to mark the swift opening and closing of his tent flap. She twisted the barrel of her Mini Maglite and swept the red-filtered beam across the camp table. Brian Griffin lay on the cot, each breath marked by soft, wheezing snores, but she ignored him.

There was a photo mostly hidden amid the clutter, a black-and-white wedding picture mounted in a sterling-silver traveling frame. Her father looked very young to be wearing an army uniform; with sword and Sam Browne belt, it struck Cass as most resembling a costume for an ill-cast play. Janet was in uniform, too, the fitted dark blue of the Royal Navy. They were standing beneath an arch of drawn sabers, Thomas's fellow Highlanders on one side, naval officers on the other. Partially obscured in the background, behind parents and best man and maid of honor, without the beard that he wore now, stood Brian Griffin.

"You haven't changed," she said quietly, but also without trying to mask her presence.

"Time touches some more lightly than others," was his reply. She'd known from her entrance that he was awake. "I was wondering when you'd notice."

"It didn't register when I was here before. I guess I was too wrapped up in myself to properly pay attention. I'm sort of amazed I didn't recognize you right off."

"Y'did, in a way."

She allowed herself a very small smile, and a nod of the head to match, at the memory as he rolled out from under his summer comforter.

"True," she said, thinking back to the Champion's Combat, and how her hand had leapt for her sword hilt at the sight of him.

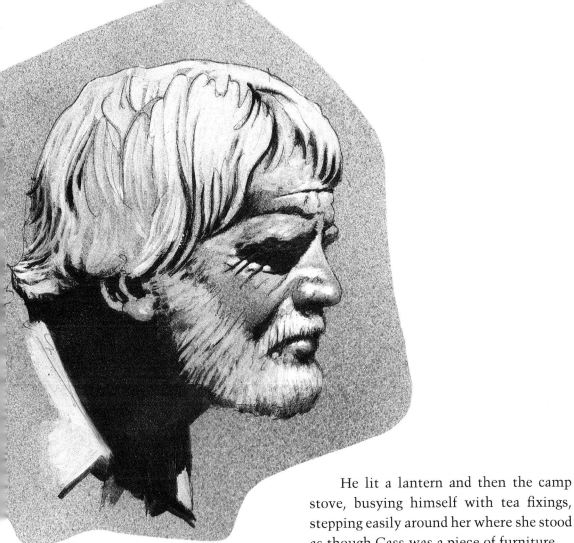

He lit a lantern and then the camp stove, busying himself with tea fixings, stepping easily around her where she stood as though Cass was a piece of furniture.

"I remember you and Daddy fighting, just before . . . that night," she said. "You'd been part of the family as far back as I could remember. I couldn't understand how things could turn so ugly. I needed someone to blame."

"Your father was a good man," Brian said, and from the set of his shoulders, Cass sensed that it was a hard memory for him, too. "But he was . . . limited. Too determined a product of the modern age."

"My parents died that night, Brian! My brother died! And I was sent away. Damn you all, I wasn't even given the chance to say a proper good-bye!"

"Fate had been tempted once, lass. It didn't seem politic to push our luck."

"Fine," she snapped, in a dismissal she didn't feel—because what she wanted, what she feared, more than anything was to know what had truly happened that night. "That was then, what about now? Why are you here?"

"For you, Cass, as I was for your father, and his before him—to try to help."

"Fat lot of good you did, old man!"

"That depends on your perspective." He wasn't fazed in the slightest by the vehemence of her attack as he handed over a mug of freshly steeped tea. "The Burning Woman could have claimed you as well. It would have been within her right."

"What the *hell* are you talking about?"

"The World, Cassandra, not as you perceive it, but as it truly *is*."

"Well, chum, I guess if I'm demented like everyone believes, I got myself some company."

"Your father had a different tone, girl, but just as absolute a denial."

"Leave him out of this! He died trying to protect me, and Mummy and Colin, too!"

"No," was the sad, simple reply. "He didn't have the sense, or the strength for that. You had enough of both to protect yourself." He looked at her. "That is the hard lesson you've been afraid to learn. It's what you chose not to remember. Ignorance"—and his mouth twisted, part with grief but part with rage at promise wasted and lives too soon cut short—"of the True Law is no salvation."

"Mharyon said"—and Cass took a breath as she confronted his words once more—"Mharyon said the War would be real."

"Do you believe him?"

"I don't . . . " She was crying suddenly. "I don't want to be a part of this."

"Then go. There's no power that can stop you."

"Gimme a lift in your Land Rover, old man, just like last time?"

"I'm here to stay, Cass. I serve Dunreith, I'm not of the Blood."

"Brian, *Jesus,* listen to yourself! They're a bunch of guys on horseback, not an army!"

"No, Cass, there are four armies here, already in place. Mharyon and his men will ride under the standard of one. They were summoned to guarantee victory, and they will do as they were bid—and their price will be commensurate with the prize.

"Aye, it's possible. I'm not sure who Mharyon is, but I know who he thinks he is, and his kind have been known to go to extremes. By your lights or mine—whether he's truly an invoked spirit or not—Mharyon takes the old rules seriously. And so should we. The fault's not his that he may be the only one present who knows them."

"It's Fieran's fight. He's King and Champion both! He called 'em, he can face 'em."

"Cass," Brian chided gently, "if he were a *true* King, he'd not have cast the summons in the first place."

"So what are we talking about, then?"

"Once the summons has been answered, you cannot simply say you're sorry, it was all a big mistake, and ask the Riders to go." And Cass had the disquieting sense that Brian was speaking from experience.

He shook his head. "Assuming you could persuade Fieran"—he offered her a smile—"and of course I have no doubts whatsoever on *that* score"—prompting a grin in return as she let herself be charmed, before he turned serious once more—"he's not a King, not their equal. He's forsworn his every oath, as you yourself have said. Mharyon would only consider the offer a greater insult."

"A Champion, then? Of the Blood? That's the only answer?"

"Aye, Cassie me lassie."

"Why does that make me want to cry?"

"I called you that, when you were barely more'n a babe. Janet said I had the knack of singing you to sleep."

"Who took care of Colin?"

"He didn't sleep. Not so's you'd notice, anyroad. For him, every moment was an adventure. He couldn't bear to miss a single one."

She stared at her mug, the tea cold and untasted, and finally faced him with eyes as haunted as his own.

"Why is this life mine?" she asked plainly.

"You're Dunreith," he said, as if that was all the answer she required. "King's Fort, in the old tongue. Protector of the Realm, Knight, Dragon Keeper—do you want to hear the rest of the titles that go with the name?"

She shook her head, one more attempt at denial. "This is such bullshit."

"Cass, we haven't time to argue. Realities must be faced and decisions made. If you're up to them."

"Well then," she said at last, and set down her mug. "We'd best get cracking."

⚜

Breakfast was light and healthy, quickly eaten. She really had nothing to say to anyone, and so she began to dress. Underpants and JogBra and old sleeveless T-shirt went on first, then a pair of buckskin trousers so snug and comfortable they were just like wearing tights. Over her head went a soft linen tunic that fell to the top of her thighs. Soft, padded Thorlo socks went over her feet, and then boots, supple with wear. She finished lacing them up, grabbed her sword in its scabbard, and then peeked out of her tent, afraid to find George waiting, hoping that Lynn or the others wouldn't see her up and about and try to cajole her back into bed.

She met Brian at the Rune Field when the sun was barely past the horizon and the field was still mostly shadow, the grass touched with dew, the distant trees laced with ground fog. A picture-postcard morning. Brian led her to the side farthest from the camp, a large duffel slung easily over one shoulder, and carrying a long, slender, padded bag that she was sure held a sword. He unzipped the faded duffel and took out a beautifully forged shirt of chain mail, handing it to her. She put it on, and found it far lighter and more comfortable than any she'd ever worn; the fit was much better than expected as well. When she mentioned this, Brian smiled.

"Faery forging, lass, and proof against the weapons of this world and the other."

Cass poked him in the ribs. "You demented old man, I think you're enjoying this way too much for my comfort!"

"Then let's just say that I've had this armor for a good long time, and I treasure it. Now don't go making it full of holes!" He turned businesslike. "Will you be wanting greaves?"

She was on her feet, flexing arms and shoulders, gauging the play allowed her by the mail; so far as she could tell, she wouldn't be any less hindered if she were fighting naked. Still, she decided against leg armor. "I can't hope to match Mharyon's strength," she told Brian. "My only assets are speed and endurance. The less weight I'm carrying, the better. Getting used to fighting in true armor is going to be challenge enough."

He nodded approval and handed her a jerkin of stiff leather overlaid with metal disks that covered the whole of her torso, explaining that good as the mail was, it wouldn't stop all blows. That was topped by a black surcoat, with a silver *dragon rampant* stitched over her left breast. The Dunreith coat of arms. She was more than surprised but said nothing. She tied a black bandanna around her neck to prevent chafing, another across her forehead to catch sweat, gathered up her gauntlets, and took a deep breath.

Brian unzipped the long, slender bag and drew out a sword unlike any Cass had ever seen. It was shaped like a broadsword but much less clumsy, elegant like a work of art. The blade had what looked like crystal for the cutting edge, and Cass

had no idea how it was joined to the steel that was the core of the blade. Looking down at the guard she saw engraved the *dragon rampant*, again the Dunreith coat of arms. Cass looked Brian dead in the eye and arched her eyebrows. He just returned the look, unblinking.

She lifted it, held it before her, testing the weight and balance. Perfect, as she suspected. She wasn't sure if she imagined things—telling herself it was merely the rising sun angling off the gleaming steel—but it seemed to blaze blindingly bright with her touch, so much so that it left its afterimage imprinted on her retina.

Knives and scabbards were left on a cloak, along with jugs of Gatorade and water and a first-aid kit. Brian wasn't in period at all, but wore running shoes, jeans, and a well-worn and faded Edinburgh University sweatshirt. He took up her poor sword.

"Ready?" he asked.

"As I'll ever be," was her response.

"Then come for me!" he barked.

And she did, only to be knocked on her ass, hard enough to hurt and bring a curse to her lips.

"Again," Brian snapped—only this time, he slammed her down even harder.

"This isn't a bluidy game," he said, his accent growing thick. "The way you're actin', you might as well meet Mharyon in a sacrifice's shift and bow yuir head to his blade, get it over with right at the start and spare everyone a lot of fuss and bother."

"What the hell d'you want, then?" she blazed back at him.

"Don't hold back. When I call, come for me as you would for him."

"You're not wearing armor or anything," she protested. "This blade could be blunt and I could still break some bones!"

"That's my lookout, Cassandra Dunreith. If you draw even a drop of my blood, you're a match for the Shadow Lord."

"Oh, yeah?" To teach him a lesson, she struck without warning, moving faster than before but at nowhere near full speed. His blade was there to meet hers and she found herself forced to spring away as his parry shifted smoothly into an attack that would have crippled her. Her blade chased his as momentum pulled him past her. She hoped to push him farther away, which would leave his side and back unprotected, but his greater strength checked hers. She brought her sword up and over in a two-handed body cut, but with a speed that matched his strength, Brian's was there to stop her, the two blades meeting with a ringing shock that sent tremors down Cass's arms and body.

"Better," Brian told her. "Again!"

She came at him every which way she knew, but it didn't matter. She improvised, she cheated, she used speed and in desperation matched her strength to his and tried to overpower him, she tried strategy, to no avail. Quick as she was, he was always quicker; good as she was, he was always better. She lost track of time and only her foreshortened shadow gave her an idea of how long they'd been working when at last Brian called a break.

She simply dropped where she stood, sprawling full length on the grassy slope, letting gravity pull her into the ground, certain she would never—could never—move again, regardless of the cause. A soft breeze brought the scent of newly cut grass mingled with wildflowers from a neighboring field, and a sudden shrill whine by her left ear told Cass a mosquito had taken an interest in her still form. She didn't have the energy even to twitch, much less bat it away.

She could hear the clatter of bodies and equipment, knew it was warriors gathering for weapons inspection, in preparation for tomorrow's Forest Battle. Marshals would move through the assemblage, making sure armor and weapons were within the assigned specifications. If you failed, you didn't fight, and since that was why a great many people had come to the War in the first place, everyone did their best and more to pass. Cass herself had done her share of last-minute improvisations with scrap leather and duct tape. Right now, she felt ready to give anything to be with her friends, laughing and carousing, comparing notes, offering suggestions, making rude threats, looking forward to tomorrow's sweaty, exhilarating fun like she did every year.

A shadow blocked the sun from her eyes. Brian, offering her the Gatorade. He let her take a couple of swallows before pulling it away.

"Vitamins," he said, kneeling beside her while she struggled up to a sitting position; she took them, washing them down with a cup of water.

"Slave driver," she muttered as he hauled her to her feet. "You realize, old man, I'll be so bloody tired after today, Mharyon won't have to fight; a breath of wind'll do his job for him."

"You're made of sterner stuff, milady," he replied seriously, though a ghost of a grin lurked at the corner of eyes and mouth; he appreciated her spunk. "Stiff at all?"

She rolled her shoulders and nodded. "The jerkin binds a little under my arms."

"Let's see." He worked a minute or so with knife and laces. "Try now."

"Better. I'm soaked to the skin. I probably stink, too."

"You'll have time to wash and change, if you want it."

"The condemned's last ablutions?"

"You think like that, Cass, it will be."

"Brian, I'm just being realistic. If I'm no match for you, what chance have I got against him?"

"Fair point," he acknowledged, to her surprise; she'd expected—and hoped for—an argument. "But the day's yet young," he went on, "and you've room for

improvement." He lunged, her blade barely parrying his attack; following the pattern established in their first hours' combat, she swung her sword up, looking for an overhand counter, only to yelp as his point touched her breast.

"Bastard," she cried, realizing how he'd tricked her, "that's *fencing*!"

When she first joined the Society and determined on a knightly persona, Cass spent two years in a professional stage fighting class learning how to use a broadsword; as a goof, she'd scrounged the time—in an increasingly more hectic and crowded and inflexible schedule—to try fencing as well. Her instructor had been impressed, lamenting that she'd waited so late in life to begin; if he'd gotten ahold of her in time, he was certain she'd have made a top-rank tournament duelist. She still visited him, albeit infrequently, and while her technique was rusty, her body remembered its cues. The only difference was that she'd been taught with feather-light fencing foils, not the double-edged hacker she was lugging now. Brian, damn his black Highland heart, didn't seem to mind a bit, he handled his far heavier blade as if it were weightless.

The first exchange, he killed her. And the second, and the third. By the time she saw the point coming, it had reached her armored breast. Finally, she matched him enough to at least cross swords, so he started disarming her. Again and again, she felt her sword twisted from her grasp and had to retrieve it from the grass, Brian's voice barking for her to "Run, run, *run*, you've no time for walking, you sotted cow!

You move like a sluggard, that's how you'll think and fight, and the Rider'll make mincemeat of you." She gave him the finger and the next time, after disarming her, he swatted her across the rump with the flat of his blade, hard enough to drop her sprawling on top of her own.

"Excuse me, m'lord," a voice called hesitantly from downhill as Cass sat up on her heels, head bent, refusing to rise until she'd mastered her temper. If Brian was trying to psych her out by making her angry, he'd succeeded, but she was damned if she'd give him the satisfaction of seeing that fury beat her. "I . . . I really hate to, *uh*, interrupt, but the use of live steel is strictly prohibited, I'm afraid you'll, *uh*, have to stop." Cass took a sideways glance at the intruder, recognizing one of the middle-rank nobility, working the inspection as a marshal.

Brian answered with his most disarming grin. "Tha' here's what y' call yuir basic demonstration o' sword combat technique, between mysel' an' my pupil." He'd broadened his accent almost to the point of indecipherability; he was taller than the Baron, and stood upslope so that he loomed over the younger man. He was resting his sword in the crook of one elbow and the sun cast the planes of his face in sharp relief, making it a craggy map of sweat-shiny highlights and shadowed hollows. There was suddenly an air of command about him that Cass couldn't remember seeing before; his clothes were modern and as ultracasual as could be, yet he projected such a presence that anyone watching could not help but obey. "It's between us alone an' none else, though others're free t' watch if the' wish, provided the' keep fair distance. Consider it on th' order of a performance."

He turned back to Cass as if the matter was settled.

"This could be trouble," Cass told him. All the Baron had to do was report them to any one of the four Kings, who could in turn order the exercise stopped. If Brian objected, they could have him thrown out of camp and Cass along with him, barred forever from the Society. Under the circumstances, she knew one monarch who'd invoke those draconian penalties without hesitation. Fieran would like nothing better than to be rid of her and this would provide the perfect excuse.

Brian made a disbelieving face. "I was dealing with bureaucrats like that lad long before you were born, Cass my love; trust me. In this, we'll be fine."

"Dunreith," came an angry follow-up call from below.

She wearily narrowed her gaze to bring the Master of the Lists a little better into focus as he made his way up the slope, leaving his subordinate behind.

"Hi, Peter," she said, assuming the worst.

"What the hell are you doing?"

"I beg your pardon?"

"Cass," Peter said, hunkering down on his heels to sit with her, "we've known each other a long time; I like to think we're friends."

"Never had cause to say different, Peter."

"But I'm Earl Marshal of the Domains. My job's enforcing the rules, to see nobody gets hurt; and you're shitting all over them."

"As my friend told your deputy, this is just a demonstration."

"With all respect, milord—" Brian began, but Peter cut him off.

"With all due respect, sir," he retorted icily, "this is between Cass and myself. You'll have your turn in good time." He turned his full attention once more to her. "I'm not wearing my chain of office, Cass, I'm not carrying my staff. This isn't official, but it is fair warning. You're *way* over the line with this. You diss my people, you diss me; you of all people should know better."

"It wasn't intentional, Peter."

"Doesn't make it right."

"Are you telling me to stop?"

"Not while you're losing, no." They both chuckled, but the moment quickly passed. "So long as you two keep to yourselves, I won't interfere. Neither will any of the Kings, although there'll probably be hell to pay after."

"You think?"

"No offense, but my life was a lot calmer the day you went strolling as a courtesan."

"You saw that?"

"I'll never tell." He sighed, and turned even more serious. "But then you strapped on your sword again. . . . There's at least one man here who would rather you hadn't. If he doesn't cause trouble, there's plenty around him that will."

" 'Will no one rid me of this meddlesome priest?' "

He nodded. "Maybe now that they're seeing what you're capable of, you'll put the fear of God in some of these young idiots, they'll think twice about hassling you." He gave her left shoulder a gentle punch. "Why don't you join us? If it's sword-swinging you're after, there isn't a company in the War that won't welcome you into its ranks."

The answer came without thinking. "It isn't fun anymore, Peter," she said simply.

"And this is?" he challenged.

She worked her stiff, sore fingers and finally shook her head. "Not fun, not exactly, but it feels right."

"I wish it were different," he said.

"You and me both," she replied.

"What you're doing here is magnificent, Cass. Don't you dare do it again."

"No fear of that, Peter. You have my word."

He nodded, slapped his gauntlets against his thigh, and strode back to his responsibilities.

Brian's shadow fell across her.

"You can still join him, y'know."

"I know," she said. "I choose not to."

He said nothing, but she sensed his approval. When she looked up, he motioned with his sword. "Shall we?"

All through the morning and afternoon they fought, Cass marveling that she could still stand, much less swing her sword. Her awareness was divided between the aches in her muscles and bones, broken by an occasional sharp burst of pain when Brian connected, and her grim determination to beat him. She didn't see that as the day wore on, her speed actually increased, the grace and power of her strokes a wonder to behold. To those watching—and there were more and more with every passing hour, few of the warriors leaving the Rune Field once inspection was done, choosing instead to observe her performance—her glittering blade left afterimages of liquid fire in the air, as she and Brian circled each other, a stillness falling on their corner of the field, broken only by the hoarse grunts of their exertions and the sharp clang of blades.

Because she'd lost all sense of time, Cass had no idea over an hour had gone by since Brian had last scored a hit, and it wasn't for lack of trying. In midattack, he shifted from roundhouse swing to fencing lunge, but impossibly she anticipated him and there followed a flurry of staccato taps as the swords danced around each other before Brian pulled back out of range. Cass, however, refused to let him disengage; she lunged for his heart, forcing him to slap her weapon aside with his open hand. She let momentum carry her forward to ram her shoulder into his solar plexus; he let out a great *whuff* that she knew was mostly faked and dropped hard on his backside, swing-kicking his legs to knock hers out from under her. But she leapt over them and brought one foot down on his sword arm, pinning it, casually bringing the point of her own blade to his throat, forcing him back until he was full length on the grass, where she had fallen when they'd first started. He grinned and opened his hand, letting the hilt fall free.

"I yield," he said, and Cass looked up in mingled surprise and alarm, really seeing the crowd for the first time as they erupted in cheers and applause.

She dropped to her knees, aware of her fatigue at last, stabbing the point of her sword into the ground and resting her hands on its guard, her forehead against the leather-wrapped hilt. She was too tired to speak, even thinking was more effort than she wanted to make.

"You did very well," Brian told her, and she acknowledged the compliment with the shallowest of nods. She knew that, she'd never been better. But she also knew that this was practice, the risk was minimal, she'd been in no real danger. Against Mharyon, she'd be fighting for her life. She tried to imagine what that would be like, how she'd feel, but her numbed brain couldn't handle the task; nothing came, neither thought nor emotion.

"What the hell was that all about?" George asked, crouching nearby—that was when she realized that everybody around her was keeping their distance. He'd come the closest and was still out of arm's reach. *Are they scared of me?* she wondered. *That's silly; surely they've seen exhibitions like this before.* But even as the thought appeared she knew it wasn't so. Very few in this crowd had ever crossed swords as she had, flat out, pushed to the wall and beyond, with nothing but your opponent's skill to keep him from disaster. She looked at Brian, understanding at last that she could have killed him—and came close to it more often than he cared to admit. He nodded, sensing her thoughts.

"You were *magnificent*!" George marveled.

"Fella," she muttered under her breath, glad to find that he was still speaking to her, "you ain't seen nothin' yet."

"But I still don't understand," he continued, not having heard her. "Why? What's the point? You two have been at it full bore for hours, with hardly a break."

"The Dunreith Diet," Cass said wryly. "It'll leave you skin and bones in no time." She climbed up the sword to her feet, groaning all the way. "I stink, Brian, I'm for a swim."

"You sure that's wise?"

"I don't really care."

"Cass?" George called after her.

What the hell, she thought, and waved him along.

⚕

She was glad for his company at the stream, when she found her fingers so stiff she couldn't unbuckle her gear. George had her stripped to her skivvies in record time, and she didn't complain when those were gone, too. While he took care of his own clothes and costume, she waved a fond farewell and toppled into the water, straight as a falling log. The current, if anything, was fiercer than ever, but she had no trouble resisting its pull. Her skin tingled with cold and it was as if all her soreness and misery was being swept out of her. She did a fast lap across to the opposite bank and was halfway through the return leg, concentrating on her stroke and the kinks in the muscles of her shoulders and back, when George cannonballed in almost on top of her. She'd never realized before that it was possible to jump while swimming—she'd never dreamed the human body could move like that, such stunts being the special province of cats and dolphins—but she did, arching and twisting like a fish, creating a pretty fair splash of her own when she landed, a face full of water making her choke.

She was coughing and sputtering too much to speak, so her response to his laughter was to shove him under, which of course only made him laugh more.

"You could've *killed* me," she screeched.

"Yes," he agreed somberly, in his best impression of Richard Nixon, "but it would have been wrong." She wanted to stay cross, but he'd nailed her again and she sagged against some mossy stones and added her laughter to his own.

"I wish I'd seen that," she said.

"Me, too. Next time I'll bum a video camera."

"Still friends, then, Kemo Sabe?"

He sidled up beside her and she didn't resist when he pulled her close. When he put his hands on her shoulders and began to knead her flesh, the sensations were so intensely luxurious she felt right then and there like she was going to melt.

"Struck a nerve, have I?"

"Billions of them. Don't stop, please don't stop."

"I've had better luck massaging steel. You used to be softer."

"It's all the practice."

"Ever wonder sometimes if there can be too much of a good thing?"

"Anne said something like that to me the other day."

"We *all* have if you'd bother to listen."

He worked his big hands off her shoulders and she curved her spine forward to accommodate him, resting her forehead on her knees. "You went straight to sleep last night. Were you avoiding me?"

"Seemed the thing to do," she told him guardedly. "I had a big day ahead, I needed my z's."

"Day isn't done, is it? I know a rehearsal when I see one, sweetheart. What's the main event?"

She said nothing, so George moved down to her feet, working them with such skill that she arched her spine until she could look at him upside down along the length of her back.

"We seem to be exceptionally limber for an old broad," he noted.

"We," she groaned, "seem to be in somewhat exceptional hands and figure we owe it all to them."

"So?" he asked, after a silence, and she knew without prompting which question he wanted answered.

"Colin was my brother," she said quietly. "He died."

"I'm sorry."

She clutched him close about her, drawing on his warmth and massive strength. "A wall from the old keep fell, killing all three, Colin and my folks. That's what I was told."

"You've never been back?"

"George, would you go back if you were me? The house is there, the land's still there, let out as sheep pasturage. It makes enough money to pay for itself, and there's a factor, a manager, who takes care of it. I've never thought about it much."

She sighed, looked at the dusk-dappled grove around them. "Until now."

He followed her gaze. "Twilight," he said softly, "magic time—Cass, I'm sorry, did I say something wrong?"

She mouthed a curse, damning herself for reacting to his mention of magic; she'd thought it the merest tremor of tension spasming across her body, but he'd noticed.

"I'm still on the practice field with Brian," she lied.

"Sonovabitch, that man swings a wicked sword. I'm glad I'll never have to meet him in a fair fight." From his tone, she knew he'd recognized the lie and she bit her lip, wondering if she should tell him. Would he believe her? She doubted it. Although George loved the War probably more than the next person, his computer programmer's mind was much too pragmatic, seeing the world in strictly binary black and white.

"What would you consider fair?"

"Him with a sword, me with a tactical nuclear device."

"That's my Rags. I do so love a man who believes in taking risks."

"Hey, you didn't see what you guys looked like."

"I can imagine."

"No, Cass, I don't think you can. I bet you can't even remember most of what you did. You put the fear of God into a lot of people; no one's ever seen you so good. I gotta tell you, I don't think you'll get an opponent for the Champion's Combat ever again."

"I should live so long."

"You have doubts?"

"They weren't supposed to show."

"We've been friends a long time, Cass," he said at long last.

"That means a lot to me, Rags."

"You mean a lot to me." She had nothing to say to that, at least that she could dare give voice to.

"I used to think I knew you," he went on.

"You don't sound so sure."

"I'm not anymore. I can't figure your moods."

"I'm past thirty, Rags."

"Like, who isn't?" he quipped lightly.

"Dammit," she flared, "I'm alone and lonely and the transitory nature of life has suddenly become painfully clear to me." She flashed her eyes away from his. "The sun's down, it's cold." She climbed out of the pool and onto the bank. He let her reach their pile of clothes before following.

"Are things that bad?"

"No, they're fine, I'm just especially cranky."

"Goddammit, don't you trust anybody? I'm no threat, Cass, I'm your friend! You're hurting, it's as plain as the fucking ground we're standing on, why the hell won't you let me—why the hell won't you let *anyone*—help?"

She rounded on him, the words on her lips: *All right, you bastard, here it comes! There are people here who want to hurt you, hurt everyone who's come for this frivolous bit of playacting we call a War. By some archaic fluke of logic, I'm the only one they'll accept as Champion for you all. Either I fight them or this whole encampment gets massacred, and I'm realist enough to know, Rags, that I really don't have much of a prayer, which means I'll probably die tonight. So help me face that, help me be brave, help me fucking* live!

But a flash of light snared her eyes, gleaming off the blade of his ax. It should have been molded rubber, but now it was steel. She stepped past him and touched its edge, snapping her hand back but not quickly enough to keep from being cut. Not even a razor was that keen. Yet, before her eyes, by the time she pressed her fingers to her lips to suck away the blood and George turned after, the ax was rubber once more, as innocent and relatively harmless as could be.

"What are you looking for?" he asked, with a manner that made her wonder if she'd spoken her thoughts aloud. "What's out there?"

"Nothing." *Not*, she thought, *yet*. She took her thumb from her mouth; there was no sign of a cut, not a trace of blood. "It's late, we'd better get back."

"You never answered my question."

"What do you want from me, George?"

"You should know."

"I've always been a loner. Maybe that's what happens when you lose your whole family so early. Nothing's solid, there's no foundation to build a life on."

She paused, struggling to put into words thoughts and emotions she was only beginning to acknowledge.

"I try to bring people close, but somewhere along the way they hit a wall I've never been able to breach. I always end up feeling hollow, missing some essential bit. I take, and take, I use, I can't give. I choose not to."

She looked at him.

"That what you wanted to hear?"

He had the grace not to answer. Cass gathered her gear, donning only the loose tunic and her underpants, and started barefoot along the path to the road. The trees had made the glade far darker than the fields beyond, the sky turned blue-tinged gray, neither day nor night.

She walked automatically, without watching where she was going. Once inside her tent, she zipped the flap shut and kicked her stuff into a corner so she'd have room to collapse onto the bed. Her breathing was short and shallow, barely this side of panic, as though she was coming off a terrific scare. Blood pounded through her skull and she buried her flushing face into the cool cloth of the pillow to try to stave off a headache. She lay and listened to the camp, voices, movements, things that had been welcome, treasured companions all her adult life. Had she been fooling herself all these years, playing roles and head games, indulging in the very things she despised most in others?

In the semidarkness she moved to the padded floor and began a complex series of stretching exercises, building on the massage that George had given her. She kept an ear out as she worked, but he didn't return; after a while she heard signs of the others taking their leave. She stretched and gently pulled every muscle in her body, concentrating solely on the physical effort, smoothing and guiding herself back into shape. Later, much later, after she finished, and was all alone in the campsite, her body was totally relaxed.

Her mind wasn't so cooperative.

She sat cross-legged on the floor, hunched over the open body of her notebook computer. She wasn't writing anything specific, merely entering whatever images and associations came to her fingertips.

She saw a reflection in the screen and thought at first it might be George.

"You don't give up, do you?" she said sourly, when she saw it wasn't.

"Stubborn as a Dunreith, that's getting to be a saying where I come from," replied Mharyon.

"Do tell?"

He filled the entrance to the tent and Cass wondered how he'd managed to slip all the way inside without her noticing. He was dressed as she'd seen him at the Barn, but while she couldn't see any weapon readily at hand, she assumed he was armed. Standing beside him was a full-length cheval mirror, beveled glass set into a dark wood frame gleaming with the double patina of age and polish. The wood was shaped into a Celtic pattern, an unending circle of running dogs. Cass told herself it was a trick of the light mixing with an overactive imagination that convinced her the hounds were alive.

"What's that?" he asked, pointing toward her screen.

"I'm writing. It's what I do."

She indicated the mirror, as he had her computer. "What do you want, Mharyon? As far as our relationship goes, it's either a little early or a little late for presents."

"Your vision appears torn between what you see and what you believe," he said. "My hope is to remove the veil that clouds your eyes and show you that both are real. And perhaps as well, a glimpse of your true self."

"I hate to disappoint you, what you see is what you get."

"Is that an invitation?"

Now it was her turn to smile, and it was a match for his, in terms both of what was known and what was promised. "In your dreams, Shadow Lord."

He laughed out loud and beckoned a hand. Cass stayed where she was and let her smile fade.

"I've seen enough of visions," she told him.

It was as though he'd seen that same thought. "This will be a better fancy, I promise," he said.

She snorted.

She sat a moment more, staring at him, trying to read some insight in his face, then rose lithely to her feet and stepped into the full view of the mirror. To stare at the reflection in mute astonishment. The face and general form were hers, but those were the only aspects that were recognizable. She wore a winged helm, but of a design she'd never seen in history or imagination. It fit her like a skullcap, flaring up and back from both temples to create the illusion that her head was elongated and not altogether human. A noseguard rose smoothly to form two oval eye sockets, which in turn flowed in a disturbingly elegant line into cheek pieces that she could swear were actually part of her flesh.

Her body was sheathed in the same material, a molded armor that

appeared to her to be some kind of lacquered ceramic—*not steel*, she told herself, *not any kind of metal I'm aware of*—that made her a shadow among shadows. It was as though she was a sable automaton, whose only signs of humanity were her eyes and the mouth that was slightly pursed in wonderment.

There was a small silver sigil on the breastplate, right over her heart, the silhouette of a *dragon rampant*.

Her gaze shifted to Mharyon's reflection and their eyes met in the glass. His image was clad in the same armor he'd worn when they met in the woods, leather and fey-forged metal, topped by a stag-horned helm. But on his face was an expression that mixed surprise and confusion; whatever he had expected to see, this wasn't it.

On impulse, she reached for the mirror . . .

. . . and gasped to find her perceptions suddenly reversed.

Staring back at her from the glass was a lean figure, all legs and T-shirt, beside a taller, broader man in midnight silk and leather.

Her first thought, as she looked down at herself was, *definitely not steel*. By rights, metal plate from head to toe—not to mention the sable chain mail she felt underneath—should have weighed as much as she. Movements of necessity were broad and exaggerated and speed became a joke. Here, though, she felt completely unencumbered.

A quick circuit told her the tent was superficially the same as hers, only minus the modern appointments.

"I'm impressed," she said as she pivoted back to face Mharyon.

"I was thinking much the same," he confessed.

"Not what you expected?" She held out her arms to give him a full court view.

"You are a woman of surprises, my lady Cassandra." He offered his hand again. She eyed it warily. "Ride with me?"

"No tricks, Mharyon," she reminded him. "You gave your word."

"No tricks, milady. I gave my word."

They emerged into twilight, the sun just gone, the sky spanning the entire evening violet spectrum with the first hint of starlight flickering above the eastern horizon. In every direction, a grassy meadow stretched and rolled toward the boundary of a virgin forest. Waiting patiently outside the tent, in the care of none other than Finn, stood a pair of chargers, Mharyon's ebony stallion and a mare whose coat was a fair match for Cass's raven hair.

"Very impressed," Cass echoed, taking in the view and the taste of air more sweet than she'd ever known.

Finn was more thunderstruck than his master at the sight of her, and Cass grinned to see him pale at her approach.

"Consider it a reflection," Mharyon told her as she swung herself, unaided, into her saddle. The horse danced nervously at first, but a firm touch and gentle words quickly calmed her. "Of your field, your forest, of your whole waking world. Perhaps even your life. A reality that might have been, or one that exists side by side with your own."

"I don't understand."

"No reason why you should." And he spurred his horse away. Cass gave a tap with her heels to send her mare cantering after him.

"This is a dream," she said emphatically, when she caught up, as though saying the words would make things so.

She got a wry grin in return. "What was it Shakespeare said? 'We are such stuff as dreams are made on.' Meaning you, milady, as much as me. But every light, no matter how pure and bright, casts a shadow. Every surface has two sides, and what you see reflected in the mirror depends on where you stand."

They reached the crest of a rise, overlooking a large pond, where a rockfall had created a natural choke point in the stream flow, to back up the water. In the distance, Cass could hear the sound of a cataract. She stood on her stirrups for a better view and saw a shimmer of silver from deeper in the wood.

"The Gates of Knockma?" she wondered aloud, settling herself once more on her saddle.

Mharyon snorted in amusement, the gust of noise startling his mount.

"Hardly," he replied.

"But if this is true, if this is home for you, then that idiot boy opened some kind of gate between your world and ours."

"It's the *same* world, lass, just different aspects."

"He said the Hunting Horn had sounded, and all the Wild Powers were loose."

"It's not his fault, Cass. The Gates are opening of their own accord, as part of the natural order of things. The boy was nothing but an instrument; the false king's transgression was to summon us through."

"They didn't know any better, how could they?"

"That's the trouble with mistakes. The first are the costliest. But also the most instructive. Next time they will."

"Stop it!" she snapped, hauling her reins to block his mount's path with hers. "You've no right to be so glib."

"We were summoned for a purpose. Falsely. By one who had no right to the claim he placed on us. The scales must be balanced."

"By a sacrifice?"

"Or a contest. If you lose, you will cross the threshold and join me. You will be bound forever to our fate and by our laws. The world you were born into will become the shadow and this the reality."

The air stirred and Cass found herself listening intently to the faintest sound of the ringing of distant chimes and with it arpeggios of merry laughter.

"My brother heard music the night he died," she said, the forest tune striking a resonant chord of memory.

"You heard nothing?" Mharyon wondered in return, bringing his horse close beside her and matching his pace to hers.

"I tried. I think I wanted to, even though Colin said I didn't. But it wasn't music to my ears, it was listening to fingernails scraping down a blackboard, it made me want to scream. This . . . is different."

"As the Seelie Court is from the Unseelie."

"I don't believe any of this."

"You do, you know, else you would not be here."

"You've a convenient rationalization for every occasion, I'll give you that."

"And you're any different?"

She was about to respond with a wicked retort, but then thought better of it.

"I suppose not," she said.

Even so, a skirling breeze stirred the tall grass and set the treetops swaying, sending dryads cascading downward to the shelter of the great trunks against the storm they sensed approaching. Mharyon cast his gaze skyward, in an echo of their apprehension, but Cass seemed oblivious.

"I meant no disrespect," he offered. "Cass." He stroked the back of her gauntleted hand. "There's a whole new world to ride here, and numberless more beyond. This doesn't even qualify as a taste."

She smiled, as much a knowing rogue as he and perhaps more so. "Is that the way of it, Shadow Lord? Are you Finvarra, come to tempt me beneath the mound of Knockma?"

"If I were my liege, lady, this would be a done deed. Only the Riders cross all boundaries. You might call us the balance between Light and Shadow, a part of both and apart from them."

He reversed his horse to bring them face-to-face, and leaned across with one hand on her saddle horn. There was a texture to his face that made her ache for him.

"You belong with us, Cassandra."

"Why are you doing this?"

"I want you."

The breeze became a wind, unnoticed on the field, as black clouds stole away what little remained of the twilight. There was no rain coming with this storm, all with eyes to see recognized that; it was something far worse. His breath mingled with hers; only a hint of a movement would bring them together, with a kiss she wanted more than anything. But it was as though her body had become the molded jet of her armor, to anchor her in place.

"Why don't I believe you?" she said, and he lost patience.

"*Damn* you!" he raged. "Are you determined to learn with my sword through your heart?"

"My thanks for the visit, Mharyon. But all of a sudden I confess I prefer *my* side of the mirror. I'll go back now."

She hauled on her reins, but he grabbed them from her hands.

"Have you heard nothing, understood *nothing*? Trust me, Cassandra, that way lies death and damnation."

"I'll take my chances."

"Would you share the fate of your father and mother and brother?"

"God *damn* you, how *dare* you!"

"You Dunreiths are as mad as you are stubborn. I want to claim you with my heart, Cass, not my blade. I beg you. Honor will be satisfied, the debt paid, all I ask is that you stay!"

"You gave your word, let me *go!*"

"I won't lose you, woman, I won't let you cast away your soul!"

A bolt of lightning exploded across the sky, flash-blinding the pair of them and startling both horses into rearing. Cass had a sense of her spirit twisting in and around itself, a duality of vision that had her looking out her own skull, but also of the body of something far greater, the creature symbolized by the helm and armor she wore. An image popped wide in her head, a name for the material that formed her shell: *dragon's scales*. Her reach encompassed the world, her perceptions the stars, and when she spoke it was with a voice that carried the weight of ages, that were and yet to be, all rolled into one.

"*I am not yours, Mharyon, Shadow Lord, to win or lose. I will go now—and you shall meet me later!*"

And in her heart, which ached still for his embrace, fire came into being, to consume her in a heartbeat and then the world as well.

🜨

She blinked, and watched an animated Mr. Spock stroll idly across her computer screen while an audio chip offered appropriate epigrams. She was sitting cross-legged on her floor, the notebook on its travel table. She kicked herself to her feet and almost pitched flat on her face as her numb legs refused to carry her weight. On hands and knees, she tumbled to the door flap, but there was no sign of Mharyon or his mirror. When she peeked outside, she found the camp fire pit and her friends' tents; everything as it was, exactly as it should be.

She turned up her lamp enough to see, though it was still very dim, the tent cast more in shadow than substance. She reached for her computer, deciding at the last instant to pick up a legal pad instead; what she had to say was better done by her own hand instead of imprinted in a machine, alongside all her fantasies.

She thought of Brittany on an almost perfect day, walking hand in hand through the haunted ruin of a castle with a man she thought she loved, in the teeth of a gale-force wind, blowing so hard they could barely stand. They'd split a bottle of malt whiskey, toasting ancient gods and ghosts and themselves; and between kisses—and groans of frustration that it was too cold, they were wearing too many clothes, to finish then and there what they were starting—they'd imagined seeing this spot in twenty years, or thirty, and how good that would feel.

There were a couple of Sobranies left in their battered, half-crushed box and she lit first one, then the last, in quick succession, hating the acrid, bitter taste—the fuckers were stale—but welcoming the momentary derailment of her train of thought. More than once she'd faced her characters with virtually certain death and, as she always did, tried to put herself in their shoes, to find through her imagination what they might be feeling and then the words that could convey it—*as concisely as possible,* she thought with a mocking smile—to the reader. Were they laughing at her, she wondered, all those creations, cheering her comeuppance?

Since before she'd started writing, she'd imagined death, lain awake at nights staring blankly at the ceiling, so scared it hurt because she couldn't face the ines- capable reality that she would someday die. To stop: no thought, no reason, a never-ending null, how could that be? She would read in papers, hear on the radio,

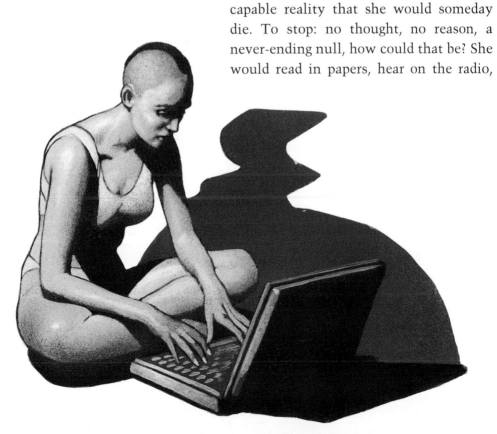

watch on TV about people whose lives were suddenly, unexpectedly snuffed out and wonder how they felt. Was there a moment, in the instant before oblivion, when they realized what was happening?

She'd never feel that aching glow that followed a really fine workout, or the wondrously special rush of excitement when an idea suddenly coalesced and she grabbed for notepad or typewriter because she couldn't keep it bottled up. She hadn't seen this morning's sunrise and wouldn't see tomorrow's. People would cry for her, not the other way 'round. She wanted . . .

. . . more than anything to have someone beside her, to have and to hold, to take her tears and give her strength; she wanted the missing piece of her life, that other self she was always told was out there somewhere.

So they lied.

So what else was new?

She rummaged in her case and came up with her favorite Danskin, daringly cut and tight as sin but comfortable nonetheless. Then came fresh socks, the buckskin pants, but instead of another linen tunic, she chose a sweatshirt. Hers was generic black, it wasn't a keepsake like Brian's, but its softness felt good and it, like the leotard, was an anchor to her life, *her* reality, rather than the one that had been chosen for her.

After lacing her boots, she slipped a knife into her left one, her weak side, but if Mharyon knew that, he might not expect an attack from there. Worth a shot, anyway. A heavier blade went onto the belt, along with the sword scabbard. The jerkin was long, reaching about an inch below her crotch, and the belt rested atop her hips rather than snug around her waist. She rolled her shoulders, nodding approvingly as the fine mail sleeves with their silk lining slid easily over her skin; she'd been worried about them binding. As she picked up the sword she paused, looking down the length of its blade. At a glance, it wasn't very impressive; the metal seemed dull, its crystal edge lifeless. How had anyone bonded two such disparate elements together, much less forged such a superb weapon? The answer, of course, was obvious: magic.

She snorted in disgust, waiting a last time for her friends to burst in yelling *"surprise"* and laughing over the magnificent practical joke they'd pulled on her. Or the doctor, to tell her gently that her mind had finally snapped itself into the schizophrenic fantasyland whence came all her stories. She was playing along, treating the night to come as real without really believing.

A hush had fallen over the encampment by the time she stepped into view. Here and there she saw campfires or lanterns, heard voices, but those few who spoke did so in muted tones, as if they were in a church. Above her, the cloudless sky was filled with stars, a sight denied her at home in Brooklyn, and the beauty took her breath away.

She gathered her caracalla cloak close about her and strode uphill, letting her feet take her where they pleased. She couldn't help watching as she went, picking out details of what she passed and saw and jotting them away in her memory for future reference. One family offered a cup of mead, straight from Ireland, and she shared their fire and songs until the cup was empty before moving on. At the Inn of the Sated Tyger, where those who'd neglected to bring their own food or simply wanted a change from campfire cooking were served, she bought mulled cider and listened to the gossip. Wars were supposed to be wilder with every passing day, but this one was exceeding expectation, to the point where some were getting actively scared.

"Pretty quiet, Tony," she mentioned to the proprietor as he brought her mug of cider.

"Noticed did'ja, milady?"

"I'm Cass, Tony," she said, "for tonight and always. I never really was comfortable with the idea that everybody here has to be nobility—milord or milady. No more, okay?"

"Whatever."

"Things really that bad?"

"Depends on your point of view. I got no customers 'cause I got no more stock. Ale's gone, beer's gone, anything with a kick, I ran out better part of the day ago."

"That's good, isn't it? You've made your profit."

"Ain't why I come here, Cass, you know that. Nor you neither." He shook his head and laid a quarterstaff on the bar. Cass had seen him conduct master demonstrations over the years; he knew how to use it. "I had to break up two fights today, one of 'em serious. There's a mood this year, everybody's got an edge, a nasty one, an' I don't like it. Soon as the War's done, I'm outta here. Gotta tell ya, I don't know if I'll be back."

She nodded agreement, then stiffened at the call of a familiar, wholly unwelcome voice.

"Dressed for war, Milady Siobhan?"

"I'm told, Philip, that's why we're here."

"She's Cass tonight," Tony said from the bar, quickly snugging his staff out of sight. "Y'ask me, suits her better. You want anything, Royal Highness? Can't offer much of a selection, food or drink, but the cider's warm."

"Cider, thanks. May I join you, Cass?"

She said nothing to encourage or dissuade him. He took that as permission and sat on the stool beside her.

"A protest has been lodged with the Council of Kings about that display you and your friend put on today. Impressive though it was, we can't abide such a flagrant disregard for the rules. You two may know what you're doing, but what about the poor idiot who gets his skull cracked, or worse, trying to match you?

"Myself, I almost had a stroke watching you. All I could think of was the publicity—not to mention the liability—if one of you got crippled or killed."

"No argument."

"You'll be asked to leave come sunup."

"I was planning to, anyway."

"We have rules, milady. We abide by them for our common good."

She gave him a glance that made him stammer and look away before saying, pointedly, "Again, no argument."

"I want you to understand," he said hurriedly. "I know we've had our differences, I know you don't think much of me . . ."

What she thought was an acid *you got that right, pal*; aloud, though, with a calm equanimity that much impressed herself, she asked, "Was I that formidable a foe, Philip?"

"I'm Fieran, milady. I'm your King."

"You're not *my* anything, Philip. What, did you think me that desperate for your crown? Were you afraid the Council would strip you of your title? Does nothing else matter but winning?"

Now it was his choice to remain silent.

"Was the title of liege lord of a pretend domain worth what you did to that poor kid? Do you have *any* idea what you've set in motion?"

"I don't know what you're talking about!"

"So you said the other night. It still rings hollow. Philip, I heard you down by the river. I've seen Mharyon and his Riders. Have you ever considered what will happen if you got the summons wrong? If they're here, not to serve your purposes, but their own?"

He was clearly, defiantly, refusing to listen, so she shrugged and made a dismissive motion with her hands.

"Doesn't matter. Done is done. Though we both may try our level best to deny it, we have to live with the consequences of our actions. For as long as we're able."

She rose to her feet, to take her leave.

"And some of us, Majesty, have to face them."

Blowing on her steaming paper mug to cool the cider, Cass made her way to the crest of the hill that overlooked the Rune Field. A marker had been placed here years ago, during the first War, to commemorate the occasion. She sat on it, leaning forward to rest elbows on knees, letting the heat of her drink cook through her gloves, wishing she hadn't been in such a hurry with that last butt.

"Straight from the Cuban embassy," George told her, handing down a slim cigar. She clipped its end and let him light it. The taste was as wretched as her stale cigarettes, but smoking helped pass the time and, oddly, relaxed her. Out of the corner of an eye, she noticed that while he was carrying his ax, he'd also clipped her Jaeger sword to his belt, along with a wicked-looking marine-corps knife; he looked like he was in garb and playing, but he'd come prepared for serious work.

"Don't stick around, Rags," she told him.

"Make me."

"Don't be difficult."

He shrugged.

"I'll move you myself if I have to."

A glance and a small, superior smile told her what he thought of that notion, and also dared her to try. She was tempted.

Instead, she said, "This is private business, Rags. Let it be. Please."

"Friends stand by each other, Cass."

"Better on occasion they should know when to leave well enough alone!"

Her flare of anger didn't seem to bother him in the least.

"So *you* say," he told her.

"If I felt there was any need, I'd have told you."

"Like, you've never been wrong before."

He reached into the shadows by his side to pull out his ax—only it wasn't a rubber facsimile any longer, but once more the honed and polished weapon Cass had seen down by the stream. He held it before him, watching the steel head flash reflections off the nearby torches and campfires, and spoke in a musing tone, as though about nothing out of the ordinary.

"And then, there's this. . . ."

"I know what I came with, Cass. I know my equipment. This is my ax haft. Now, either someone switched heads on me—literally in the few split seconds I was looking the other way—or we're ass deep in the Twilight Zone."

He hammered the ax down onto the ground, burying its head in the earth.

"I don't see Rod Serling anywhere about, do you?

"Anyway, I did some thinking and I figured that, because you're so shit-scared, whatever's going on must be serious. And I figured finally, if that's the case, you'd damn well better have someone to watch your back."

"Rags, you don't know what you're saying."

"Could be. Doesn't change anything. Here I am. Here I stay."

Without heat, without emotion, too drained to argue any longer, she said, "Fuck it. Fuck you."

To which he companionably replied, "Fuck you, too."

Minutes passed. "What are you looking for?" George asked, following her gaze over the field and into the black forest beyond.

"Warriors on horseback," she said simply.

"You're serious!" She said nothing. "She's serious," he repeated as if by saying the words again, he could convince himself that his friend hadn't just gone nuts. Except, that would mean she was telling the truth, which was even more insane.

Cass was well into her second cigar when an indefinable change in the air told her it was time. The moon had risen, its lower edge just clearing the horizon, the sight warped by atmospheric parallax so that Earth's satellite appeared far closer and larger than it truly was. The air was cool and absolutely still. Cass had the feeling that the only movement was caused by the soft swirl of breath in and out of her lungs. All was silence; even the rumble of trucks down the interstate was muted and faraway. A look over her shoulder brought a half smile to her face: George was sitting cross-legged, ax hooked over his shoulder, head lolling onto his great barrel chest, deep asleep. Five thousand people within earshot and she'd lay any odds only one other besides her was still awake.

She heard a flash of cloth overhead and saw a standard take the breeze, emblazoned with the same sigil she wore. Brian held it steady, with an ancient air about him that belied the sweater and dark corduroys he wore, as though he'd been doing this—standing by his knight and liege—a thousand years and more.

When she faced the field again, there they were, facing her in line abreast a hundred yards away. Even though she was staring down at them, she had the sense that they were somehow looming over her, dominant, malevolent presences too formidable for her to resist. They were of an age when Man and the World were new, when Life and Death were identical mysteries and the great powers flowed in everything. Wild creatures for a wild time.

Well, fuck 'em; so was she.

There was a savage yell behind her, but she didn't take her eyes off Mharyon as a charger thundered over the crest of her hill. Peripheral vision recognized the shape of the helm as Finn's. He had a man's bound hands thrown over his pommel, forcing him to match the pace of his horse. When he reined in, sheer momentum propelled the prisoner forward as though he'd been shot from a catapult, pitching him off his legs and facedown at Mharyon's feet.

With a wild-eyed mix of fury and fear, Fieran scrambled for dignity and footing and failed to find either.

"How dare you," he squawked. *"How dare you!"* But none of the Riders—their leader least of all—paid him the slightest heed.

Cass stayed seated as Mharyon dismounted and strode toward her, responding to his courtly bow with a curt nod.

"I and my folk have come for what is rightly ours," he announced, his host murmuring growled agreement.

"And I ask, Lord, that you depart in peace," Cass answered.

"What are you doing?" Fieran cried. "*I brought you here, you should be talking to me!*"

"A fool summoned you," Cass continued, ignoring Fieran's increasingly vocal outrage. "It was unintentional, an accident; surely in your hearts you can find the charity needed to forgive?"

"Lady, we are said to have no hearts. And a false summons, by forsworn knight and false king, is an insult not so easily excused."

"Are you so proud?"

"No less so than you. It is because of ignorance this crime cannot be pardoned. A lesson must be taught. We and the powers we represent must *never* be taken lightly. The sacrifice of the many, or willing offering of the one.

"The choice is yours, Lady. Which is it to be?"

"My god," cried Fieran, understanding at last the parley, fearing they spoke of him. "*My god!* You can't be serious!"

"Be silent, fool," rumbled Finn. "For the offering to have meaning, it must be worthy. You're not even close. Your life, *all* your lives, they're in her hands."

She stubbed out her cigar and shrugged the cloak off her shoulders, rising to her feet. She didn't have to see Mharyon's face to know he was smiling in appreciation, or read his mind to realize he was already imagining her riding the shadows at his side. Perhaps she could turn that cocky arrogance to her advantage; anticipation had screwed more than one sure play.

She wished she'd paid more attention in church; the only prayers she remembered had to do with school, teachers, and passing tests, and they were invariably denied. She unhooked her scabbard and laid it on her fallen cloak, pausing a moment to stroke the rough wool, as if saying good-bye to a trusted companion.

"Thou wert a comelier lass when first we met."

"If you're in the mood for romance, bub, I'm sure something can be arranged."

He laughed, honestly amused, and wished aloud that fate permitted the alternative. And then he matched her bare sword with his own.

She held hers in both hands, point angled up and a little to the side, almost like a baseball bat, while Mharyon's was close to his leg, as if he couldn't be bothered to lift it. Being upslope of him gave Cass equal height, at least for the initial blow. *Christ*, she thought, *he's bigger than I remember, and he probably dances in that bloody tin suit better than other people do naked!*

Faster than her eye could follow, he swung his blade up and overhead, cutting straight down in a two-handed stroke that would have split her from collar to crotch had her own sword not jumped to meet it. The impact jarred Cass to her toes as she rebounded to parry his next attack. He seemed to come at her from every direction, without even a pause for breath, the two of them hammering, hacking away, standing virtually toe to toe, neither giving an inch. It was a display of brute, stubborn force, and by rights, Mharyon should have won. *Adrenaline,* she thought, *endorphins.* And then, as she divined his pattern, she suddenly ducked, his sword whistling uselessly overhead, throwing him a step off balance; she was too close to get a decent shot with her own weapon, so she hurled herself into him instead. As she'd expected, his armor protected him—she probably felt the impact far more than he—but she succeeded in making him lose his footing. He flailed, feet slipping sideways on the dew-slick grass, and crashed down on a knee. Cass sprang at him, only to move as quickly back, hiss-cursing in pain from the cut he'd opened in her thigh. The bastard had switched hands and proven himself as talented with the left as the right. The wound was messy and hurt like the devil—her pants were ruined, too—but it was only a surface scratch, not a liability. For the present.

This first exchange done, they circled each other, keeping their distance; the Shadow Lord had grown wary, respectful of Cass's skill, and she knew the moment she underestimated him would be her last. He stepped toward her and she gave ground too hastily, aware as she did that he was forcing her toward his horsemen. She muttered a curse at how easily he'd seized the high ground; now, the advantages were tumbling his way. *What to do if he charges me,* she wondered, expecting the move the moment she thought of it, *duck and run, or try and meet him?*

He bellowed from deep in his gut, a shocking explosion of raw sound that froze her in place a split second; for that instant she couldn't think and didn't react, in that moment he came for her. With sick desperation, knowing it was too little too late, she parried, only to see her sword spin out of her grasp; but as it left her hands she kicked aside, diving and rolling away from the fallen blade—the opposite of what he'd anticipated she'd do—and his follow-up strike missed. It wasn't a smooth recovery, her cut leg didn't have the power she needed, and the burst of weakness threw her off stride.

She decided to emphasize that, trying to make Mharyon believe the injury was more serious than it appeared. She'd drawn her belt knife—the blade long enough to qualify as a short sword—and managed to parry his next attack. To her dismay, though, she saw chips in the bright Jaeger steel; the finest forging she'd ever seen, and it was nothing compared with Mharyon's blade. He lunged for her heart—the opening she'd prayed for—and she spun down the blade, almost into his arms, stabbing her knife into his chest, screaming in frustration as it snapped against his armor. She clawed for his eyes, then, forcing him to throw her aside—but not before she'd drawn blood of her own.

She landed hard enough to drive the breath from her lungs and saw her sword a few body lengths away. She kicked herself into a flat dive, her hand closing on its hilt the same second Mharyon's own knife buried itself in her back. It was as if ice and fire had been poured simultaneously into her body; she went cold and yet she burned. She couldn't seem to draw a decent breath and knew it was because a lung had been punctured. She reached behind and snagged its pommel, biting back a shriek of agony as her effort widened the cut, managing to yank it free and collapse onto her back just as Mharyon loomed overhead, his blade crashing down onto the X formed by her sword and the knife he'd thrown. He hacked again, with all his strength and fury. Another strike would separate her arms from their shoulders. Cass didn't intend giving him the chance. As he reared up, so did she, her weakness and awkward position combining with his armor to deflect a certainly fatal blow. But the counter had the desired effect, driving him back far enough to enable her to regain her feet. Her back was sodden—*Pity*, she thought, *that isn't honest sweat*— and each breath filled her mouth with the metallic taste of her own blood; she could feel tiny bubbles of froth on her lips as well. It was then she realized she was dying.

Strange, but that took away all her fear. She'd crossed the Rubicon. No longer could her imagination torment her with dreams of what might be and fears of leaving—losing—what was; before too long, she'd know. She crab-crawled uphill a few steps. That was really all she could manage, the gentle slope had suddenly become a sheer cliff and her feet would no longer stick to such walls, and beckoned to Mharyon. *C'mon, hotshot*, she dared silently, *show your stuff. Come for me.*

He did, and she met him one-handed, her left clawing her reserve blade from her boot to slash it across his face, opening him from cheek to chin, barely missing the eye. He howled—more in surprise than pain—but had no chance to properly recover as she followed him, using both weapons to harry and cut, to hurt and possibly maim rather than kill, to whittle him down to her size instead of going right away for the home run, the perfect blow that might win—or lose—all. She had time for that, she'd make it!

Then he punched her, a backhand that left her head ringing and cost her a tooth; she used the momentum of the blow to spin herself around, but it was the wrong side, the wrong blade, and he caught her knife in his glove and tore it from her grasp before hitting her again.

She found herself downhill of him, and try as she might, she couldn't stop him drifting in and out of focus; she was sure that last fist had concussed her—now that she knew what it was like, she resolved not to be so cavalier about heroes in her stories giving and taking such punches, and then she laughed at the ridiculousness of that thought. She was done with stories. She'd tried her best, but there didn't look to be any upset tonight; the favorite was sure to win. She let that realization sink into her muscles and bones; her shoulders drooped ever so slightly and the sword shook with the faintest of tremors, for all her grim-faced efforts to hold it steady.

"Lay it down, Lady," Mharyon called. "I swear your end will be quick and without pain."

"No," she told him, her whisper followed by a hollow, racking cough that brought up more blood. *I must look a goddamn mess,* she thought.

"Your choice," he said, and attacked for what both knew was the last time.

She waited until he was committed, the blade already arcing toward her head, and then fell backward in a judo roll, grabbing the front of his tunic and pulling him with her while kicking upward with her good leg to bowl him all the way over. Somehow she managed to hold on as he landed, the momentum pulling her up on top of him, sitting hard on his stomach, a fierce grin on her face as she heard his startled breath whoosh out of his lungs. She stomped on his sword arm with her good leg. She tried to pin the other arm, but that side of her wasn't up to the job. He had a second knife and it bit deep into her side. By then, however, she was already rising to her feet, crystal sword inverted in both hands, held as high as she could reach above her head, above his chest.

With a cry torn from her soul, she rammed the blade through his armor into his heart . . .

. . . and collapsed on top of it.

How long she lay there, Cass didn't know. After a time she became aware of a cool breeze caressing her cheek where the air had been still before, the preternatural quiet broken by birdsong and the faint burp of frogs in the lake. Mharyon lay still beneath her, eyes wide, face marked with disbelief. *Fancy that. I actually caught the sonovabitch by surprise.* She lay her fingers over them as gently as she could and pressed them closed.

From the base of the slope came the snuffle of horses, the chink of gear, and Cass pushed against the hilt of her sword, in a vain attempt to shove herself erect. It was as if her body had become carved stone, it wouldn't be moved, no part of her would obey her will. So she tried again, and again, and that third time stone came to life and she made it to her feet, crystal sword in one hand, Mharyon's blade in the other.

The line of warriors hadn't moved, they stood watching impassively. Cass wondered what they felt: resentment, hatred, respect? She'd killed their captain, did that mean anything? Were they free, or would they choose another to lead them? Were they even bound by their slain lord's word; for all she knew, they might be duty-bound to avenge him. That'd be cute—a feather would finish her; tickle her nose, induce one decent sneeze, and Cass Dunreith would be history. What the hell, she had no right to be standing, breathing, speaking now.

"The price," she said in a hoarse voice, so soft she wasn't sure she even spoke, "is paid. Scram. Now."

"If you have no objection, my gracious lady," Mharyon said from over her shoulder, "I would greatly appreciate the return of my blade. It has served me well and I would miss it dearly."

She couldn't help screaming, stumbling around and nearly pratfalling, except that he caught her.

"You . . . !" she stammered like an idiot; this was impossible, simply had to be, she could see the hole in his breastplate where she'd thrust her point home. "I . . . !?!"

"We of the Shadow Realm do not measure existence as you do in your waking world; there is little in a time and place of magic that cannot be undone."

She didn't believe this; the creep was going to walk away—she'd won the battle, saved everyone, was going to drop dead any second, and the sonovabitch she supposedly killed was getting away scot-free! "No fair, bastard, no fucking way!" She raised her sword arm, only to realize belatedly that he'd plucked both blades from her grasp and handed them to a mounted lieutenant. "Is this an example of your word, Rider; the game is played by your rules until you lose and then you rewrite them so you win instead?"

"Ignorance, your name is Dunreith. Listen to yourself, my lady, is not your voice somewhat stronger than a moment ago? Breathe deep, do you feel pain?"

She didn't. He wasn't holding her all that tightly, either; she found herself standing virtually without help. Cass slid her tongue over her teeth—they were all there—and then reached through the slash in her clothes to feel skin that was smooth, unmarked, untouched.

"Neat trick. Pity I can't do this more often."

"Why not? You have the power."

"What do you mean?"

"You are Dunreith, heir to Ca'rynth, and all that entails. There is little in the realm and ways of magic you cannot do; for such as you, milady, a hurt done by magic is most easily dealt with."

"You're serious!"

"And you have much to learn—about yourself and the true world." He looked around, nodding absently to himself, as if he was seeing not the camp as it really was, but as the life and times and beliefs it represented, and Cass felt strangely sad. She thought of all the stories she'd read about gods and spirits who'd outlived their age and found themselves cast from reality into legend, and of how she'd feel if it had happened to her.

"My words are barely spoke, and already you have completed your first lesson," he said, stroking her cheek with his fingertips, almost a lover's caress. "I would stay and talk more, but your bright blade has broke the string that bound me here and I and mine must flee once more to our shadows."

"I'm sorry," Cass said, and to her surprise, meant it.

Mharyon threw back his head and laughed. "Glad I'd have been to claim you to my side, Cassandra, but gladder still to fall before you. Time enough for you to ride with shadows; for now, you're better suited to the sun." He mounted as he spoke simply, "I do believe we shall meet again."

"Next time as pals, okay?"

In reply, he handed down her sword; the moment she touched the leather-wrapped hilt, it blazed with silver fire, casting Cass and all around her in absolutes of light and darkness. By rights, it should have revealed Mharyon's face as it did her own, but he remained eerily in shadow within his helm. Her expression was questioning, a little confused. To herself, she felt achingly, clumsily young, as she hadn't since school, while his face remained hidden. Friend or foe, she hadn't a clue. Which meant, probably both.

Suddenly Mharyon looked past her; Cass turned to follow his gaze and beheld Fieran, forgotten in all the excitement, standing by Finn's charger. He was staring saucer-eyed at her sword.

Finn's horse shouldered him forward, and he staggered toward Cass like a man going to the execution block, his face more like a death mask with every halting step.

He dropped to his knees before her and spoke in a rushing whisper, words repeated over and over, as though it was some mantra he prayed would save him.

"I'm sorry. I'm so sorry. I didn't know, how could I have known? I didn't mean any harm. Please, I'm sorry. I'm sorry. I'm so sorry."

He raised his eyes to hers, but saw no mercy in them. He lifted his crown from his head, staring at it dumbfounded to behold that it was a real crown and not the costume facsimile he'd been wearing all week.

With trembling hands, he offered it up to Cass in an acknowledgment of fealty.

She took it from him, one-handed, and stared grimly at it. Crown in one hand, sword in the other, as though weighing the two. Then, with a convulsive heave—and such a cry of mingled grief and rage that Fieran scuttled away from her like a crab, in terror—she hurled the crown away.

The light of her sword faded. She let her shoulders slump, as though the night's exertions had finally caught up with her. She looked around for Mharyon, but he and the Riders were gone.

She stood alone on the field.

Off in the distance, a trucker sounded an impatient air horn—yelling, no doubt, at some sluggard car blocking his lane on the interstate—and she heard the faint roar of a jet high overhead. She sought in vain for its navigation lights, then slowly climbed the slope to where her erstwhile champion sat dead to the world. She sheathed her blade.

"Oh, Rags," she breathed, hunkering down by his side, "you should have listened when I told you to stay away." She leaned toward him, and kissed the top of his head. She sniffed, using the heel of her hand to wipe her eyes; the relief was temporary, her tears wouldn't stop coming.

Brian offered a handkerchief, and then a ring of ancient silver, with the figure of a *dragon rampant* etched onto its flat surface.

"The Dunreith signet," she remembered, from her father's finger.

"Worn by the Laird of the Domain since the days when the world was young. The formal title is Duke—in your case, Duchess—of Ca'rynth."

"Suppose I say I'm not interested."

"Your privilege. But Cass, you cannot deny what you are. The way of the world has changed, is changing, will continue to change.

"Forces and powers banished for better than a thousand years are abroad once more in the land. There are precious few among humankind with the sensitivity to even know what's happening, much less cope.

"Your father—rest his poor damned soul—denied that birthright, and by so doing condemned himself and all his family save you. He refused to believe, even when the truth cut the heart from his body."

Cass closed her eyes tight and clutched a fist to her chest as though to crush the signet she held.

"A thousand years an' more I've served your family, Cass Dunreith," Brian said, "as my father did before me, an' his before him! I've loved, an' seen those I love die; I've seen your ancestors forswear their duty, and rush to embrace it; I've known cowards and heroes, the worst and the best. Tell me it's cruel and arbitrary and unfair of the Fates to cast you in this role, I'll not argue. It's the way of things.

"But you have the Gift, child, as it's not been seen in the Dunreith line since James, in Plantagenet times. You are the Black Dragon."

"Whatever the hell *that* means."

"You'll learn."

"I need time, Brian, to be by myself and think."

"I'll look after your gear and make appropriate apologies."

"Yeah." She rose to her feet. "What about the boy who started this all?"

"In saving the camp, you saved him, too."

"Hooray for me. This was a *game*, Brian!"

A sudden gust of wind snapped a King's standard out straight from its flagpole as she waved her arm to encompass the camp and all it represented.

"But how can I play when I've known the real thing? How can I pretend to fight, when I've risked my life and shed my blood? How can I live the fantasy"—she slipped the signet onto her left ring finger and closed her hand tight, smiling thinly to find the ring a size too large—"when I've known reality? The terms don't have any meaning anymore, not the way I've always known them.

"This was important to me, Brian, and now it's dust. I'm done here. I can never come back."

"I know, lassie. I'm sorry."

"What's worse is that I'm afraid it may be the same for George. Each in our own way, we've both seen beyond the glamour of this war. My 'Blood' got me into this mess, his only excuse is that he cared for me. It's a shitty way to pay him back.

"Take care of him, will you? Until I sort out what's what."

"As my lady commands."

"I'll call when I'm settled."

"We'll be waiting."

With a last look around, Cass strode over the crest of the hillock and on up the path, the way she'd come only hours—a lifetime—before. Her thoughts were inward—her mind faraway—yet her eyes never rested and her right hand was always free, ready to draw her sword on a moment's notice. Behavior that had been an affectation a day before was now instinct, the playactor had become a warrior.

At her car, as she unbuckled her sword belt and laid it in easy reach on the passenger seat, she paused and looked around. Something in the wind had caught her ear, a faint rumble—like thunder, only alive—the roar of some great, impossible beast. In the east, the sky had begun to glow, but the west was still dark with night. The horizon was lined with clouds, and her eyes widened and she caught her breath as they seemed to flow into a discernible shape. She saw a head and neck and body, and wings that stretched to the ends of the earth. An ebony dragon, its scaled flesh glittering with the lights of the universe, its flame heralding the dawn. It looked down at her, its wings beating once and sending a wind across the field that shook the tents and bent trees yet did no lasting harm; it bared its teeth and roared, and Cass swayed as she realized the voice it spoke with was her own.

She twisted the signet a little so she could see the seal, the ring a perfect fit—as if it had been made for her from the very beginning.

And, in truth, perhaps it had.